What's a **D0729036** *finds herself i*

If she's with the right person, the possibilities can be absolutely **mind-blowing!**

Don't miss another sizzling installment of one of Blaze's most popular miniseries:

24 Hours: Blackout

#612 JUST FOR THE NIGHT
by Tawny Weber
(May)

#620 MINE UNTIL MORNING
by Samantha Hunter
(June)

#626 KEPT IN THE DARK
by Heather MacAllister
(July)

24 Hours: Blackout—
No lights. No power. And no holding back...

Dear Reader,

Summer is here, my favorite season, and I am
thrilled to be part of the Blaze 24 Hour: Blackout
miniseries (be sure to find Blackout books by
Tawny Weber and Heather MacAllister!). In
Mine Until Morning, Jonas and Tessa spend a
stormy night in a Philadelphia blackout. Blackouts
have a way of bringing people closer, and
Jonas and Tessa become *very* close during their
adventure.

Jonas is also suffering his own personal blackout
due to his recent blindness, but being in a blackout
levels the playing field as he helps Tessa cross the
city of Philadelphia in order to help a friend. Jonas
also has three gorgeous brothers—all of whom will
have their own stories, so keep an eye out for my
upcoming Berringer Bodyguard books.

Animals are a huge part of my life and often
appear in my books, and *Mine Until Morning* is
no exception. I hope you enjoy meeting Irish, the
feline partner at the Berringer Bodyguard Agency!
To find out more about him, be sure to check out
blazeauthors.com, and learn all about our new Pet
Project!

Happy summer,

Samantha Hunter

Samantha Hunter

MINE UNTIL MORNING

TORONTO NEW YORK LONDON
AMSTERDAM PARIS SYDNEY HAMBURG
STOCKHOLM ATHENS TOKYO MILAN MADRID
PRAGUE WARSAW BUDAPEST AUCKLAND

Recycling programs
for this product may
not exist in your area.

ISBN-13: 978-0-373-79624-3

MINE UNTIL MORNING

Copyright © 2011 by Samantha Hunter

ABOUT THE AUTHOR

Samantha Hunter lives in Syracuse, New York, where she writes full-time for Harlequin Books. When she's not plotting her next story, Sam likes to work in her garden, quilt, cook, read and spend time with her husband and their dogs. Most days you can find Sam chatting on the Harlequin Blaze boards at Harlequin.com, or you can check out what's new, enter contests or drop her a note at her website, www.samanthahunter.com.

Books by Samantha Hunter

Thanks to Julie Dutt,
for help in understanding scent, soap-making,
how to set up Tessa's soap shop, and for
the great soaps she makes to go with my books.
Check her out on Twitter: @latherati.

Many thanks to Diana Holquist and Madeline Walsh
for help with Philadelphia specifics. Particularly
thanks to Diana for info about the Fletcher St.
Urban Riding Club that matches inner city youth
with rescue horses, inspiring the appearance of
one of Philly's Urban Cowboys in the book.

Many thanks to Eileen
at SEPTA Customer Service in Philadelphia, for
quick, friendly responses about SEPTA Blackout/
Emergency policies and city route information.

And to Mike,
much love and thanks for everything, as always.

1

JONAS BERRINGER FLIPPED the Closed sign on the door of the soap shop, Au Naturel. For the ten hours that the shop was open, all he could think about was being alone with the owner, Tessa Rose.

It was a swelteringly hot Philadelphia evening, which was the norm lately. Though it was cool in the storefront, the air-conditioning making it cool where he stood. Plain wood shelves were artfully stacked with every color and scent of soap and lotion he could imagine. Small baskets of samples, lip balms and various other trinkets and testers were placed strategically where customers would find them.

It was classy, elegant and yet still somehow warm and inviting, much like Tessa herself. Aromas of what he now recognized as jasmine, sandalwood, orange and vanilla, among others, filtered through his senses.

The back room wasn't air-conditioned, and a blast

of heat hit him as he walked into the small foundry, the workroom where Tessa made her products.

It was a little bigger than the actual store and twice as pungent. He'd gotten used to it though, and it didn't seem overwhelming anymore.

Several tubs and two stoves took up almost all of one wall, and there were shelves of wood soap molds and various containers, amber vials and tools there, as well. On the other side of the room, shelves of curing soaps lined a wall next to a refrigerated unit where more perishable supplies were kept. There was a table for cutting and wrapping next to the desk where Tessa did her accounting.

"Jonas," she said, her pretty blue-grey eyes warming as she looked up before he announced his presence. He knew that she'd been waiting for him, too. They'd been dancing around this, around each other, for several weeks. Now, it was finally going to happen.

He closed the distance between them, oblivious to the slippery coating of lotions and oils slathered on her hands; she'd been working. He didn't care about the mess as he pulled her up against him.

"Jonas!" she exclaimed with a laugh before he covered her mouth with his in a hot kiss that left no guessing as to how hungry he was for her. He walked her back until she was pinned between him and the table behind her. She moaned, pressing tight against him, returning his passion kiss for kiss.

Jonas buried his face in her neck. "You like driving me crazy, don't you?" he accused playfully, nipping her earlobe.

Tessa had always been hands off. The boss's daughter. A woman way out of his league. But being around her 24/7 for the past weeks had pushed his control to the limit, and now all bets were off.

She sighed against his cheek as he nibbled at the soft lines of her throat, and then pulled away.

"I've been trying my hardest. I thought you'd never give in," she said with a sexy smile. "You and that iron control of yours."

"You have too many clothes on," he said gruffly.

Continuing to smile at him in that minxlike way she had, she wiped her hands on a nearby cloth and slid the smock from her shoulders that she always wore while making her soaps and lotions.

Underneath, there was a simple yellow sundress with a halter top tied around her very graceful neck. When she reached up to hang the smock on a hook by the worktable, he could see her delectable shape outlined underneath.

He wanted to touch and kiss every inch of her.

"I'll be right back. I need to lock up," she said, sliding him a glance, still playing. Tempting him. Making him wait.

"I already did. We're alone. Come here," he said.

"You're so demanding," she murmured, returning to his arms.

"Desperate for you is more like it," he whispered against her lips.

"I like the sound of that," she purred. "And I feel the same way."

"I can't get you out of my head," he confessed, his arms sliding around her.

His hands shook with the effort to slow down, reminding himself that Tessa was a woman to be cherished. A woman *he* cherished.

He gasped when she nipped at his lower lip with her teeth, apparently rejecting his gentle approach.

"Don't hold back, Jonas," she said in clear invitation, linking her arms around his neck.

He swallowed hard, sliding his hands up over her slim arms and shoulders, tugging at the halter tie. Her eyes became smoky, her nipples hardening under the thin fabric.

"I'll give you whatever you want," he promised, and he meant it. "Whatever you need."

"Just you," she said, sending his pulse racing.

He pushed the dress down until her pretty breasts were bared to his view. His eyes moved over her as if unable to completely absorb how gorgeous she was. Taking a peach-toned nipple between his fingers, he pinched gently, then soothed and pinched again, watching her head fall back, cherry lips parting, the pulse in her throat pounding.

She tugged both his hands up to her breasts and covered them with her own, squeezing. She was so openly sexual, it mesmerized him.

"*More,* Jonas," she said, making his cock jerk in response.

Gentleness was forgotten in the wake of desire that took him over. Her apartment was right upstairs, her bed just seconds away, but that was too far, too long to wait. He'd take her here, as he had been fantasizing about for days.

Tugging the rest of her dress away, he pulled her up against him for a deep, hard kiss that made them both breathless, his hands everywhere. Over her shoulder, he perused the shelf of oils and ingredients, breaking the kiss to reach back for a bottle of sweet almond oil.

Dropping a light kiss to her neck as he poured

the rich-smelling oil in his hands, and smoothed the slippery-soft substance over her skin. He started with her slim shoulders, strong from the work she did, but still so delicately shaped. Then he worked his hands down over the slope of her back and hips. She leaned back into him with a sigh when he slid around to her front, where he spent long minutes massaging her breasts until her head dropped forward and a small moan delivered from her throat.

She was like a piece of sensual art, a perfectly sculpted woman come to life under his hands.

"Jonas, this all feels good, but I need more," she said, pulling away as she turned to face him. She stood before him in nothing but slight, yellow satin panties, her skin gleaming where he'd worked the oil over her. "You have no idea how much I want you," she said, looping her thumbs into the scrap of material and sliding it off until there was nothing between them.

"I think I have some idea," he whispered, taking off his own jeans and shirt. She walked into his arms and they were skin to skin, finally. The satisfaction of it was mind-boggling.

He ran his hands reverently over her thighs, the rounded globes of her ass, the curve of her hips. His erection jutted against her, eager and needy.

"I want you, Tessa," he said, his breath catching as he kissed her.

"Then take me," she invited with a sultry gaze.

He reached for an open jar of honey she had forgotten to put away and dripped golden dollops on her breasts then licked them off. As he finished, she was shuddering and straining toward him, her nails digging into his arms.

His hand slid under her knee to pull her leg up around

his hip, his cock brushing against the silky, wet flesh he wanted to bury himself in.

"Jonas, please," she begged. "Now."

"Not yet…let's make it last," he said. As much as he wanted her, something bothered him. There was something about the light in the room that didn't seem right. He looked around, making sure they were alone.

A lingering sense of dread held him off for a few more seconds.

What was wrong?

Nothing.

Tessa moved against him, oblivious to any problem.

But it was his job to protect her. That was why he was there in the first place, her hired bodyguard. There had been some threats against Senator Rose and his family, and Jonas had been more than willing to keep an eye on Tessa. In fact, he'd found it difficult to take his eyes off of her.

He glanced around the foundry once more. Nothing was out of place. He was imagining things, and turned his attention back to the woman in his arms.

Words evaporated for long, steamy moments as Jonas gripped her hips, lifting her up completely against him so that he could plunder her mouth as he thrust forward, planting himself deep inside her welcoming body. She was hot, tight, and they fit perfectly, as he knew they would.

She pulled back, watching him as he thrust into her. He could tell when she bit her lip, her eyelids fluttering shut, long lashes brushing her cheeks, that she was close.

He found a steady rhythm and tried to focus on every nuance of her as he held her. Small sounds came from her throat that were sexier than hell, her mouth forming a perfect O as she trembled and started to careen over the edge.

He bent to suckle a breast, flicking his tongue against her hardened nipple. That small touch pushed her over. A soft scream fell from her lips, her body tensing and pulsing around him as she came.

Jonas wanted to join her, but he needed more, thrusting faster, harder, focusing on the heat of her body, how soft her skin was under his hands. Her inner muscles fisted around him tightening and releasing again as she writhed in his arms, and he moved faster.

The satisfaction he'd craved was so close it was almost torture, but he couldn't quite get there. His body burned as he drove himself into her, precariously hanging on the edge of the orgasm of his life.

Tessa leaned back in his arms, watching him curiously, her expression serene, happy and satisfied, but somehow distant.

"My father is not going to be very happy about this," she said, sliding her hands up over her ripe breasts, smiling at him. The room around her became hazy and unreal in a way that made him squint.

Then she became transparent, too, the tight heat of her body fading.

"No, wait, please," he cried out, reaching for her.

The golden light around her was fading. The acute emptiness, the ache of satisfaction denied made him gasp in agony, chilled now, shivering.

He was alone. Only darkness remained.

JONAS SHUDDERED WITH cold as his eyes opened, unseeing, but awake nonetheless. He was sweating and the AC was blasting directly on him. As he rolled to the side, he swore as his foot tangled in a sheet and nearly sent him sprawling on the floor.

He was still hard from the dream, and even the cold blast from the AC didn't seem to diminish the ache between his legs. His body jerked as he remembered Tessa's imaginary touch. The emptiness that always followed the dream was an ache in his chest.

Providing his own release wasn't an attractive option. It wasn't an orgasm he craved; it was Tessa.

He had to get her out of his mind or he was going to go crazy. He supposed it was his punishment, a special little kind of hell, for letting himself get distracted from his job. He'd been assigned to protect her, not have sex with her.

He should have turned around and walked out the first time he entered the shop. When he saw her, it was like being set on fire. Jonas had had plenty of women in his life, but none that made him want at first sight. Not like Tessa.

Senator Rose was responsible for sending Berringer Security several contracts, particularly after Jonas's younger brother had successfully prevented a kidnapping attempt on the senator a few years earlier.

James Rose had even become a friend of sorts. When he'd asked them to guard his daughter after receiving threats concerning a bill he was authoring, they couldn't refuse. The senator had trusted Jonas to keep his daughter safe, and he'd done a rotten job of it. Not one of Jonas's better moments.

Jonas did the usual background checks, and he knew about Tessa's reputation going in. The senator's "wild child," Tessa was a free spirit, nonconformist. She was also heart-stoppingly beautiful and completely off-limits.

Father and daughter had a tumultuous relationship, to say the least. From what Jonas had seen at a distance, Tessa looked like one more spoiled rich girl who liked to rub her father's nose in her exploits. He'd known plenty of that particular type over the years.

Tessa had made several questionable choices in relationships, among other things, that seemed more about thwarting her father's control than anything else.

However, Jonas discovered that the view up close was somewhat different. For one thing, Tessa wasn't a girl anymore, but a mature woman who ran a successful business. As he got to know her, he couldn't help but see her in a different light, though he knew her relationship with her father was still troubled.

Getting in between the senator and his daughter was dangerous. Jonas had to pick one side or the other, and he chose the side that paid the bills. Besides, he knew too well how that kind of slip could come back and bite you in the ass.

Guarding Tessa had been a little more intense than his usual assignments. They'd been around each other 24/7 for several weeks, almost constantly together. He didn't let her out of his sight, day or night, as per the senator's orders. It made it harder to control the heat that had flared between them.

Tessa wasn't big on control, and she tempted his from every angle she could. One night, when they'd returned from a party, he'd given in, right in the parking lot behind the store.

He'd watched her all evening, dancing with friends in a dress that had been molded to her, what there was of it, anyway. A few of the friends she'd danced with had been male, and it made Jonas want to claim her as his in a very basic way.

Ridiculous, but true.

Her sharing even an innocent dance with another man had driven him crazy, and by the time they'd returned home, he couldn't hold back any longer.

He was so distracted that he hadn't noticed someone watching them from a dark corner of the lot.

The guy had approached from behind while he had her in his arms. A hard slam to the head had knocked him out. Tessa had fought back and, admirably, had taken out the intruder with a bat she kept in the back seat of her car.

Jonas had awakened at the hospital later, completely blind.

The senator's aide, Howie, was the first voice he heard after the doctors told him about his condition; apparently Rose wasn't available.

From what Howie said, it was clear Tessa had told them that Jonas had screwed up big time. He was off the job. Worse, she'd made it sound as if *he* had been pursuing *her,* and that he had seduced her that evening, instead of keeping his eye on the target.

She'd clearly used him to piss her father off for sending a bodyguard in the first place. He'd known she wasn't happy about the idea—the senator had warned him—and she hung him out to dry. He should have seen it coming. That he'd fallen for her added insult to injury.

Jonas had never liked Howie Stanton, but Howie was a Washington insider and had been with the senator for years. Jonas had noticed on more than one occasion when the senator had come to Tessa's shop how Howie's eyes followed Tessa. His expensive suit and high-profile position didn't make him any less of a lowlife.

But Howie had made the senator's wishes clear to

Jonas: stay away from Tessa, or there would be consequences. Jonas could hear in his tone that the aide
relished delivering the news.

Jonas did as the senator requested.

He hadn't seen or talked to Tessa for a month since
the attack, and he didn't plan to. He'd played the fool
once, and it wasn't worth the risk to Berringer Security's
reputation. The senator could do them a lot of damage
if he wanted to.

Feeling for the edge of his bed stand, from which
he knew it was about seven steps to the window, Jonas
found the AC unit. After a brief struggle with the curtain and the controls, he managed to turn it down to
low.

After getting a cup of cold water from the kitchen, he
found his way back to the bed. Traffic was busy down
on the street, people going about their normal lives. The
apartments on his floor were quiet, everyone gone to
work.

He picked up the basic clock that one of his brothers
had bought him and removed the glass cover so that he
could feel the hand positions.

One o'clock in the afternoon. He'd always been an
early riser, but now he slept whenever he could and
woke at odd hours.

His brothers, Garrett, Ely and Chance, were running
the business without him until his sight came back.
Doctors said his sight *would* return, but it hadn't.

What if it didn't? What if they were wrong? The chill
that ran over him had nothing to do with the AC.

The hard hit to the back of his head had left him with
a concussion and severe bruising to his optic nerve,
causing temporary but complete blindness. The dura-
tion of "temporary" was unknown. Doctors had no idea

when his vision would return. He'd seen four specialists, all offering the same fuzzy explanations of the mysteries of the brain.

Be patient, they'd said.

He shook his head, running a hand through hair that he'd let grow too long. It bugged him, especially in the heat, but he didn't feel like hearing the questions and sympathetic comments from his barber or anyone else. So he'd holed up here, mostly, waiting for life to return to normal.

Jonas reached to the left, groping to find his cell phone, and he held it in his hand. Thankfully, his was an older model with a hard keyboard that he could still use, though he sometimes hit the wrong button.

He still had the number for Tessa's shop on speed dial, number two, second only to the office, and he ran his thumb over the button, as if tempting himself. He should erase it, but couldn't quite do it.

Cursing, he put the phone down and found his way to the shower. As much as he wanted Tessa, he'd get over it eventually. His blindness made things worse, blowing his attraction to her all out of proportion. He was frustrated and bored. When he had his sight back, he'd be able to move on, get his own life back.

Maybe the hit on the head had kept him from making an even bigger mistake. At least the attack had happened before they were both naked, out in the open for anyone to see.

No sooner had he turned on the water when he heard a knock on the front door—soft, but he could still hear it. He'd always had sharp senses, even before he was blind. You didn't survive in his line of work without them.

Still, there was a noticeable uptick in his perception

that would have been kind of cool if it weren't at the expense of his vision.

"Keep your pants on, I'm getting there," he said as the knock sounded again, harder this time. He wrapped a towel around his waist and shut the water off. It had to be one of his brothers, come by to pull him out of bed, no doubt. He had another doctor's appointment that afternoon. It galled him not being able to go anywhere on his own and that he required help for everything.

It had to be Garrett, who had been fussing around him like a mother hen since the attack. Jonas made his way to the door, opening it and turning to walk back into the room.

"I know, I slept late, but the appointment isn't for another hour. Give me a chance to clean up, then we can go," he said.

"Jonas?"

He stopped in his tracks, frozen. He wasn't dreaming now. He didn't think so, at least.

"Tessa?" he said, his voice choked and not sounding like his at all. He turned toward her voice, knowing this was real as the familiar scents of honey and almond filled the room. His heart slammed in his chest.

"What the hell are you doing here?"

"WELL, THAT KIND OF greeting sure makes a girl feel welcome," Tessa Rose countered with no small bit of sarcasm, hoping to cover her nerves.

She took a deep breath, in part for courage, and in part because seeing Jonas for the first time since the night of the attack had knocked the breath right out of her.

He'd lost some weight, his dark hair grown out from military short to longish, brushing the tops of his shoulders. He was clad only in a very small white towel, slung low on his hips and slipping lower. She found herself licking her lips, and tried to push back the lust that always erupted when she looked into those dark eyes.

Something was off, though.

He'd looked right at her when he'd opened the door and then turned away, talking to her as if he had expected someone else. That told her the worst of it.

"You're blind," she whispered, her voice stolen by her surprise.

"Yeah."

She saw the change in his body language, the way he tensed as he turned his face away from her, his jaw tight. He was wounded and embarrassed about it. Ashamed to be caught this way, exposed and vulnerable.

"I didn't know."

"Your dad didn't tell you? Oh, right, I guess you pissed him off royally, so he's probably not confiding in you these days."

She drew back at the bitterness in his tone.

Tessa had resisted the notion of having a bodyguard at first. It was reflex for her to resist her father. He was a great politician, she knew, but a total control freak, and he liked to control her life more than he should. It was an understatement to say they hadn't gotten along, and they still had their problems, though things had changed a bit since her mother had passed away two years before.

The senator manipulated everything to the benefit of his image, a necessity of his political career, he always claimed. Tessa had grown up resisting his control, and she'd be the first to admit that she hadn't always done that in positive or productive ways. But then again, her father hadn't always played fair, either.

As she got older, they had hammered out a truce of sorts, but mostly because she lived in Philadelphia where she ran her business—and her life—the way she wanted to, and he stayed in D.C. They got together on holidays, and it was enough.

When he said he was sending a bodyguard to her shop, they'd argued, but she'd relented when she sensed he was really concerned. He seemed to think this particular threat was very serious—and it had ended up that way.

She'd expected some stiff in a suit, but then Jonas had walked in the store, over six feet of muscle, brooding eyes and sensuality all wrapped in well-worn jeans and a bomber jacket.

Every bad-girl instinct she had surged to the fore.

The feeling she had when she was with him was like that zing of perfect chemistry that she always experienced when she made a new scent.

Scent was the most primal of the senses. Complementary scents attracted or enhanced a relationship, and the wrong scent repelled. It was the most basic principle of natural chemistry, the basis of most elements of survival. She and Jonas were a perfect combination, she could tell from the moment they locked eyes on each other.

Jonas obviously hadn't agreed. He kept his distance, his treatment of her businesslike to the nth degree, but she saw the desire in his eyes when he thought she wasn't looking.

That only upped the challenge. Tessa didn't give up when she saw something she wanted. To that extent, she was very much like the senator. She wanted to make her bodyguard lose that rigid control. It proved to be more of a challenge than she thought, until that night in the parking lot.

She'd met her friends for a birthday celebration— not hers—and she'd worn the sexiest dress she owned. Jonas didn't think she should go, but she told him that she was going, and if he wanted, he could tag along. In truth, she'd dressed for him. Danced for him. Tempted him in every way she knew how. And she'd almost given up—the man seemed to be oblivious—until they arrived home. He didn't say a word the entire drive back, but then hauled her against him as she'd stepped out of the car and kissed her until she couldn't breathe.

When she'd felt the hardness of his chest pressed against hers, she didn't back away. He didn't, either.

His wonderful hands had been sliding up under-neath the sheer fabric of her gown, holding her backside against his hardness, his masculine scent surrounding and seducing her like a drug, when it had all gone wrong.

"We shouldn't be doing this," he'd whispered against her neck as she'd let her hands explore him the way she'd been dying to for weeks. He was a big man, in more ways than one, and her body craved him.

"Maybe that's why it feels so good," she'd replied, and she would remember the lust that had burned in his eyes until her dying day.

They were completely wrapped up in each other when the attacker hit Jonas from behind. He'd dropped from her arms to the pavement, leaving her to face her attacker, a political extremist who clearly was willing to cross the line to protest her father's work. Tessa still could feel the icy fear of that moment, thinking Jonas had been killed and that she was next.

She'd gotten very, very lucky, remembering the bat she had in the back of her car from summer softball games with her friends. Adrenaline served her well in fighting the man off.

She figured at first, when there was no word from or about Jonas, that he was just laying low. Staying out of the limelight, since the story had been all over the news, at least insofar as her and her father were mentioned. The Berringers might not have existed, which is what she supposed made them effective.

From her experience, some protective details, she knew, were all about the flash. They wore Armani and soaked up the media attention that guarding famous or powerful people granted them.

Berringer wasn't like that. They were serious security who put the client first. When she tried to find out about Jonas on the web, she'd found next to nothing; there were a few news articles from when he was on the police force, and the agency web page, which offered a minimum of information.

The Berringer brothers in the background, keeping their clients quietly safe.

It soon became clear that Jonas wasn't just laying low. He didn't want anything to do with her.

Her father was caught up in business on the Hill when the attack happened, and Tessa kept her distance from Howie, who was holding court in her father's absence. Tessa didn't ask Howie anything about Jonas, since she didn't want to encourage her father's aide. Howie had come on to her a few times, and she'd made it clear that she wasn't interested, but the guy didn't seem to understand the word *no*.

Jonas's brothers wouldn't tell her anything, either. She assumed that they all blamed her for distracting him and almost getting him killed. Rightfully so. She'd tracked him down now, intent on apologizing, but she hadn't expected this.

"I'm so sorry, Jonas," she said on a raw whisper as she dragged her attention back to the present.

He looked fierce as he closed the space between them. He might be blind, but Jonas honed in on her with no hesitation, his hands clamping hard over her shoulders.

"Stop it, Tessa. Sympathy is the last thing I want from you, or anyone."

"What do you want, then?" she asked, her mind trying to grasp the new discovery.

"What I'd really like is for you to go, and don't come back," he said harshly.

She lifted hands to frame his face, and he flinched, but she didn't draw back. No way was she leaving.

"What happened between us that night, Jonas, it—"

"Meant nothing," he interrupted. "Why are you here? Haven't you done enough?"

"What do you mean?" she asked, shocked by his tone. "I came here to apologize—"

"Come on, Tessa. Your father made it clear that you didn't want a bodyguard in the first place. He said you could be…difficult. So, what? Was getting me into bed the easiest way to piss the senator off and get me pulled off the job? Or was it just for fun? Were you bored?"

"None of that is true," she said, appalled.

"What happened that night shouldn't have. I take full responsibility for that, but I won't make the same mistake twice. You should go."

His obviously low opinion of her hurt more than she

imagined it would have. Did he hate himself that much for giving in to her? For wanting her?

"The way I remember it, you wanted me as much as I did you, Jonas."

He paused a second too long before nodding shortly. "It was a momentary lapse. It happens sometimes when mostly naked women throw themselves at you," he said unkindly.

"I see," she said, stepping in and tracing her finger down his chest, feeling his heart slam under the hard wall of muscle, and her own heart thudding even harder. She was angry, hurt and intent on not being so easily dismissed.

He was perfect. His skin was deep brown from the summer sun, taut and warm with a sprinkling of dark hair that provided softness over the hard cords of muscle that flexed under her touch. There wasn't an ounce of fat on him. Her fingers played over the sculpted muscles she had only fantasized about.

His hands grabbed at the air, seeking and then finding her wrists, holding her away. A pulse throbbed in the base of his throat. He wasn't unaffected by her at all.

"Stop, Tessa. No more games."

"No, Jonas," she said softly, not fighting his hold, but leaning in as she lifted her mouth to take his unsuspecting lips in a warm kiss. "No more games."

He resisted, standing rigid, his mouth firm and unmoving, until she sighed against him and licked at his lower lip. She inhaled deeply, loving the manly scent of sandalwood, soap and sweat. "You make me crazy. You know it's true."

He cursed against her lips. His hands tightened on her wrists, but then let go and his arms banded around her and pulled her in, his mouth opening to hers, taking control, plundering and ravishing her in a hard, punishing kiss.

Tessa gave herself up to him, let him take his fill as she took hers. They parted a few moments later, both breathless.

"Is this what you want, Tessa?" he asked when he pulled back, and she paused before responding.

He was hard, his arousal clear under the towel he wore. Not immune to her, not completely.

Or was it how he said, that any man would respond this way?

"Not like this," she said, seeing none of the warmth or desire in his face that had been there before.

He shook his head in disgust. "You know the thing that really ticks me off? That you would come here, intent on getting whatever it is you want, with no regard for the consequences to others. You don't care who gets hurt, do you, as long as you can stick it to your old man."

"I never did that. My father respects you, or he wouldn't have sent you to guard me. And he and I don't have that kind of relationship anymore."

"Right. As if you couldn't wait to rub what happened that night in his face. I'm the hired muscle, after all, not the guy he'd want you to end up with. That he sent me must have been icing on the cake."

"He has no say in the matter, but I didn't—"

"If you came here for more, forget it. I'd rather you don't use me as a way to make that point to him."

"What's between us has nothing to do with my father," she said, frustrated.

"There is no us."

"There could be."

"Not gonna happen," he insisted stubbornly.

Tessa stepped back, stinging at his rejection, but refusing to accept that there wasn't anything between them.

"Well, in case you decide to change your mind, you know where I am. But I wouldn't wait forever, Jonas."

She walked out, and he didn't say another word.

2

THE NURSE IN his ophthalmologist's office had bumped against Jonas four times while showing him down the hall to the office, and then again in the office itself. She sounded cute and smelled nice, like jasmine and vanilla. She was also stacked, from what he could tell when she leaned past him as she'd opened the door.

As the door opened and the doctor came in, she leaned close and pushed a piece of paper into his hand, whispering, "Call me. Let's have a drink sometime. I can show you some tips for getting around without your sight."

"I'll bet you can," he'd said with a chuckle, but in truth it left him completely cold. All he could think of was Tessa, and cursed her again for her earlier visit.

He didn't even know how she'd gotten his address, but he supposed a senator's daughter had good resources. It paid to know people in powerful places—until you pissed them off.

"Hey, Doc," he said to Dr. Matt Sanders, his eye

specialist, whom he'd known in the Philadelphia business community and their basketball league for some time, though never as a patient.

"Jonas," Matt acknowledged from somewhere to the right and stepped in closer. "I hope you don't intend on answering my nurse's invitation," he said lightly, lifting one of Jonas's eyelids to look.

Jonas didn't pull back anymore, having gotten used to the closeness, as well as the poking and prodding around his eyes.

"Do you see anything? Flickers, shadows, flashes?" Doc Sanders asked.

"Nope, nothing," Jonas said, trying to keep his voice level. "Why shouldn't I call her?"

Matt chuckled lightly. "She's trying to make me jealous. That's why she waited until I was in here to slip you that note. Probably nothing written on it."

"I see. You two are—"

"Jury is still out," Matt said.

"So how does it look?"

"I'll probably ask her out, see how work mixes with pleasure. I don't want to lose her as my nurse. She's very good."

"I meant my eyes," Jonas said dryly. "No worries, Matt. About your nurse, I mean. I'm not interested in getting involved with anyone right now," he said. "She's all yours."

"Gee, thanks," the doctor replied, poking at Jonas some more, going back and forth between shuffling papers and checking his eyes.

"Any headaches? Nausea?"

"Nothing notable."

"Okay, well, it's looking much better. The swelling is almost completely gone, but it's the bruising that's probably causing the ongoing problem. That can take some time. If there's no progress in a few weeks, we'll run more tests, see what's up."

Jonas sat perfectly still, but his hands turned cold. Matt's voice was so neutral, that particular doctor tone that tried not to upset patients, but just made you all the more paranoid. Not that it took much these days.

"Do you mean this could be permanent?"

"No. Really, Jon, if I thought there was a serious possibility of that, I'd tell you straight up," Matt reassured, and Jonas breathed again when the doctor put a reassuring hand on his shoulder.

Jonas wasn't a particularly touchy-feely sort of guy. He and his brothers all had their ways of sharing physical contact—including fighting—and his family was probably more or less as affectionate as most. But since losing his sight, touch had taken on a completely new meaning. He welcomed it, and at some particularly dark moments, even craved it.

Matt continued, "The nervous system is delicate and unpredictable, and everyone takes their own time to heal. Your brain will let you know when it's ready to let your eyes work again. Give it a few more weeks, and if you aren't back to at least partial vision—and it's very likely you will be—then we'll figure it out, okay? Be patient. That guy nearly cracked your skull open. This could have been much, much worse."

Jonas nodded, grabbing on to the "very likely" bit with both hands. He'd always considered himself a patient guy until recently. First Tessa and now his eyesight had proven differently.

"All right, Doc," he said, standing and running his hand along the wall to the door. "I'll wait and see."

"You take care, Jonas. Let me know right away if

there are any changes. Make another appointment for a check in two weeks on the way out."

"Will do." He found the knob and opened the door. "Doc?"

"Yes?"

"Your nurse. She's getting impatient."

"What makes you think that?"

He rubbed his fingers over the paper in his pocket. "There is writing on the paper. I can make out at least three numbers," he said, handing the doctor the note and leaving Matt to think about that as he made his way out to where his brother Garrett waited for him in the lobby.

"What's the verdict?" Garrett asked. Jonas could hear the worry riding under his casual tone as they made their way out to the car after Jonas made his follow-up appointment.

"Same. Everything looks fine. It just takes time. Hopefully things will start working again within a few weeks, or they'll do more tests to see why not."

"Damn. Well, we have to stay positive. Things could change at any moment."

"Yeah, no reason to think otherwise, for now." It was easier to say it than to believe it.

"Smart man."

"Smarter than you," Jonas joked, delivering a solid, friendly punch to his brother's upper arm, nodding in satisfaction as he felt the solid muscle of Garrett's tricep under his fist.

"Pretty good aim for a blind guy," Garrett joked.

"Watch it or I'll aim higher," Jonas returned.

It was good to laugh about something. What other choice was there? Their family had seen their share of hard times, growing up on the lower end of lower working class, even though his parents had worked like dogs to provide their four boys with everything they needed. There were various crises along the way, always handled together with humor and love.

This was no different. His lack of vision made Jonas feel like an outsider, different, even with his own clan. People treated him differently, and he didn't like it.

"So she just walked in?" Garrett asked out of the blue.

Garrett had shown up as Tessa was leaving, bumping into her as she left the building. Jonas had been raw and completely unable to discuss the visit at the time, so Garrett had let it go, let him calm down. He still didn't want to discuss it as his brother led the way out to the car, but he knew Garrett wouldn't let the matter drop.

"Let's get some food. I missed breakfast and lunch," Jonas said, and then blew out a breath before answering the question. "Yeah. She just walked in."

"I knew I liked her," Garrett said, and Jonas could hear the smile in his voice. It was a new experience, hearing smiles. "I know *you* liked her, too," Garrett added, pulling away from the curb.

Jonas didn't answer. His brother was a romantic.

Lust had very little to do with liking someone, in his view, but he had to admit, he had seen a lot to like about Tessa while he had worked with her for those few weeks. More than he had expected to. More than he was comfortable with.

She was dedicated to her business, much as he was to his. Her obvious caring for her customers and her friends was clear, and she did seem to truly love her father, in spite of their differences. She was extroverted, sexy and gregarious, but not the reckless, selfish woman he had envisioned. At least, that was what he'd thought until she'd proven him wrong.

There were a lot of reasons to keep a principal—the term they used for the person receiving their protection—at arm's distance. Women in particular, even married women, had a tendency to fall for their bodyguards—a kind of transference, like falling for their doctors or therapists. Jonas never took the bait. Not before Tessa.

"You know what she did, Gar. She didn't have to tell anyone what happened between us. It was my bad for falling for it in the first place."

Garrett couldn't argue that. Losing a client like the senator was a major blow.

"I think you should give her the benefit of the doubt. She came by the office a few times, looking for you, and I don't know, Jon. She just didn't hit me that way. There might be more going on."

"How else to explain her father warning me off her?"

"I guess you have a point. But you were different when you were around her for those few weeks. I can't put my finger on it, but I thought she might be good for you."

"Frankly, after what you've been through, I'm surprised you have a romantic bone left in your body, Gar."

Jonas heard his brother's silence louder than any reply, and cursed under his breath at his blunder. "Sorry. I shouldn't have gone there."

"It's okay. You're right. Lainey and I had some wonderful years, and I lost her too soon. But what we had was great. You deserve that with someone. You're too much on your own all the time."

Rain was coming down a little harder than when they left, and Jonas remembered that some strong storms had been forcasted for later in the evening.

Jonas didn't respond, but his brother's words hit home.

They were different men, even if they were brothers. Garrett had lost his wife in a car accident while he was gone on a job, and it had nearly wrecked him. He'd bounced back, and from what Jonas could see, would be able to find happiness again someday. Jonas hoped he would. Garrett was made for family, being a husband, a father.

Jonas didn't see that in his future, but he still put family first. The senator's aide had made Rose's threat clear—if he went near Tessa, there could be serious repercussions to the agency, to Jonas's brothers and everything they had worked for. No way would Jonas risk that.

"You should come in the office today, listen up on some of the recent cases," his brother offered, changing the subject.

"Maybe," Jonas replied.

He'd like nothing better than to get to work, but he worried about being at the office too often. He figured it was better to keep his condition as hidden as possible. If clients discovered he had messed up or been seriously wounded on the job, it could compromise people's confidence in the agency, in their ability to do their jobs.

The car stopped, and Jonas detected the rich aroma of cheese steak and onions from their favorite shop just west of Center City.

"This way," Garrett directed, walking at his side. Jonas negotiated his way along with the cane, hating every minute of it, but he needed it to find his way through more obstacle-ridden environments like streets and crowded public places. As soon as they reached their table, he stashed it away.

"It's just a cane, Jonas. A tool. People don't even notice. Most blind people these days live very normal, active lives."

"I'm not a blind person. This is temporary," Jonas bit out, and then regretted his tone.

Garrett was right, but Jonas was edgy—an understatement of the emotional mess Tessa had left him in.

It had taken everything he had inside not to take her to bed right there and then. He was that hungry for her, and that fact generated even more self-disgust. How could he be so attracted to a woman who was obviously so manipulative? But if she hadn't said no, he knew it would have happened.

It was just pent-up lust and frustration, or so he told himself.

His lack of vision certainly hadn't seemed to put Tessa off any, he thought, remembering how passion and need had practically vibrated off her. Her scent was still on his skin. He didn't know if she was faking that or not. The senator was out of the country, and maybe she'd decided to finish what they'd started when her father was out of play—something like eating cake and having it, too.

"Well, if not with Tessa, you still need to get out more," Garrett continued. "You're blind, not under quarantine. When was the last time you were even on a date?"

"Now, there's the pot calling the kettle black," Jonas accused.

"I've gone on a few dates, but my situation is different."

Jonas frowned. "I don't *date*. I have plenty of women I know who are available when I want one."

"Classy."

"Drop it, Garrett. Can we talk about cases, the weather, anything but this? You're beginning to make me wish I'd gone deaf, too."

Garrett laughed and acquiesced as their sandwiches arrived and they dug in. They were delicious as always, though Jonas was getting a little tired of sandwiches, in general. They'd been standard fare since he lost his sight, as he didn't have to worry about using utensils to find the food on his plate, or embarrassing himself in front of others.

When his sight returned, he was heading for the first Italian restaurant he could get to for some pasta. Ideally, he would meet one of the women he called now and then to join him and kill two birds with one stone. If he could get back to his normal life, he knew his obsession with Tessa would fade.

"We're supposed to be getting some wicked storms today. It's already turning gray out there. The news said there were tornadoes down south, and it's all moving this way," Garrett commented.

"We could use the rain. Get rid of some of this heat," Jonas said. He loved summer storms, the power and energy of them. "What are Ely and Chance up to?"

"They're both in the field. Ely's finishing up the bank job down in Norfolk, and Chance will be caught up in New York for a while. Ely should be back tonight, depending on how the storm affects his travel. I've just been minding the store."

They always tried to have three in the field, with one

in the office. They alternated home duty. They didn't want a secretary, and Garrett did the books. The fewer additional people in the agency, the tighter the security, and that was what it was about.

Ely was the most serious of the bunch, the second youngest, a Marine and just returned from a lengthy tour in Afghanistan. He'd almost re-upped, but after recovering from a near-fatal injury caused by an IED, he'd decided to come back home.

Jonas had held his breath with the rest of his family for pretty much the entire time Ely was gone, and was never as relieved as when his little brother came home for good and joined their family venture.

Chance, aptly named, was their baby brother—and hated being called that with a vengeance. He was also the risk-taker of the family. If it could launch him over a cliff, speed him around a track or take him thousands of feet over the earth, Chance was up for it.

He was also a crack shot and a martial arts expert. Jonas always told him he was overcompensating for being youngest and two inches shorter, though at a solid six feet, it hardly made a difference. In so many ways, easygoing Chance was more deadly than all of them put together because he seemed to have no fear of anything.

"Another couple of jobs well done," Jonas murmured, proud of his brothers and wishing he could have felt as happy about his own work recently.

The Norfolk job, in particular, was one that James Rose had recommended them for. A high-profile case at a federal bank, it was a nice feather in their cap.

Not only had Jonas crossed a line almost sleeping with Tessa, but if anything had happened to her, he'd never have been able to forgive himself.

He was quite sure the senator would never forgive him, and Jonas only hoped that in time, they could still do business together.

He and Garrett made their way back out on the street. The air was even thicker than before, the humidity near smothering, though a warm wind blew around them. He could hear thunder in the distance rolling closer as wet drops splashed on his face.

"So what now?" Jonas said.

"I have some paperwork stacked up at the office," Garrett said, walking along.

Jonas was faced with the paralyzing anxiety he'd had every day since coming home from the hospital. When he couldn't work, he didn't know what to do with himself. He used weights, listened to books, listened to TV, which was maddening. There wasn't much he could do at the office.

He didn't like being at loose ends, useless to those around him. His thoughts and emotions tangled in the darkness that was his life at the moment as they got in the car and drove slowly down the city street. Heavy raindrops hit hard on the outside of his brother's car as a heavy gust of wind shook them.

Garrett started to say something when a crack of thunder and lightning boomed around them, and Garrett hit the brakes hard.

"What happened?" Jonas asked as they stopped cold.

"Tree down," Garrett said, sounding apprehensive. "Just split and blocked the street right in front of us. This is getting bad fast. The office is closer than your apartment, so let's head that way and hunker down there."

Jonas murmured agreement, his thoughts still on Tessa, though they shouldn't be. The humid air made her scent rise from his skin, and he swore he could still taste her from the kiss they'd shared that morning. The electric energy in the air from a nearby lightning strike seemed to exacerbate the memory.

He turned on the radio, listening to the storm warnings, trying to forget her, though he suspected it was going to take a very long time for that to happen.

"I SWEAR, LYDIA, I had no idea. It was such a shock. How could they not tell me that he's blind?" Tessa asked for the fourth time, pacing the hard tile floor of the foundry, her voice breaking with misery. "And it's because of *me*. My father had to know. He could have told me."

It was starting to rain harder, the drops falling more heavily from a blackening sky; even though it was only midday, it looked like evening. The weather approximated her mood.

Lydia Hamilton, who owned the tattoo shop Body, Inc. next door to Au Naturel, looked on in sympathy as Tessa paced.

"Your dad has been traveling, and you know how he is. It's not your fault, Tessa. These guys take risks every day," Lydia said in her usual frank fashion. "It's part of the work they do. It is a shame though. He was hot."

"He still is. He's blind, not maimed or dead," Tessa said, thanking the universe for that, at least.

It was part of why she always resisted the protection her father pushed on her. She could never stand to think someone died trying to protect her. What made her so special?

"Jonas was so…angry. He has some idea that I was using him to get back at my father."

"Well, that was your M.O. once," Lydia said, sliding her a knowing look.

"Yeah, back in my twenties. Not for a long time. Believe me, it didn't take long to figure out the jerks I dated to annoy my father didn't make me happy, either. I can't figure out why Jonas would think that. We got to know each other quite a lot in those few weeks. I thought he was starting to like me." More than like.

"Well, he's lost his sight. It's a trauma. People have strange reactions to things like that. Maybe he just had to strike out at someone, and you were there."

"I guess. But he was pretty specific about why he was angry with me."

Never had Tessa imagined the degree of Jonas's injury from that night. She remembered feeling reassured when she'd heard his voice as he talked to the EMTs when they had loaded him into the ambulance. She'd wanted to go with him, but the police wanted to talk to her about the attack, and then her father had sent Howie to check in on her, and everything was chaos for the rest of the night, with the press and trying to get rid of Howie.

"Are you sure he's angry with you? Maybe he's just upset in general?"

"*Furious* might be a better word."

"Well, maybe wait it out, see what happens. He might come around."

"I guess I shouldn't have pushed the issue by throwing myself at him. If he had a bad opinion of me to start with, that didn't help. I was just so hurt. By how he kept saying there was nothing between us."

"So you wanted to prove that there was."

"Yeah."

"I don't know. From what I saw, the way he used

```
(H)RX#  6333450                    10.00
SUBTOTAL                           10.00
TOTAL DUE                          10.00
CASH                               10.00
```

```
06/15/11   16:43   MIM   00303349 01
```

ZBOSNIK, SHEILA A   ZBOSHE

(H) -- FLEXIBLE SPENDING ACCOUNT ITEM

****

to look at you, a fool could tell he was crazy for you," Lydia said, picking up a lotion sample and rubbing it into her hands, then smiling as she sniffed.

"I like this," she interjected. "Is it new?"

"Yes. I meant to tell you about it—it's a combination of gardenia extracts and spices."

"Nice."

"Well, I put the ball in his court. I told him if he wants me, he knows where I am. I'll be damned if I'll beg or humiliate myself any further."

"Under the right conditions, I might consider begging if a guy like Jonas was interested in me," Lydia said mischievously.

"You're a bad influence, you know that?" Tessa said, smiling at her friend.

Lydia smiled sympathetically, which accentuated the small crescent moon tattooed at the corner of her lips. "So I've heard. If he's smart, he'll show up at that door and apologize. If he doesn't, it's his loss. You have to be able to move on."

"I know." Tessa sighed. "I just never really felt with any other man what I felt with him."

"Then you haven't been with enough men, my friend."

"Again, the bad-influence thing."

"I have to get back to the store," Lydia said, looking upward as thunder crashed louder outside, offering Tessa a warm smile before she walked to the door. "I do love storms. I know you don't. If you need company, just text me. I'm closing down early."

"Okay," replied Tessa as two other people walked into the store.

She didn't expect any business in weather like this,

and the two women struggled to get their umbrellas folded and left their raincoats on hooks by the door.

"Welcome to Au Naturel, ladies. You are a couple of determined shoppers, to be out in this weather," Tessa said with a professional smile, helping them set their soaked umbrellas by the front window to dry.

"We had no idea the weather was going to be this bad, but we had to stop here before heading home," one explained, pushing a handful of thick, auburn curls away from her face, smiling.

"I'm getting married this weekend, and I need to buy some items for my honeymoon. You know, maybe some scents that will drive him a little crazy? A friend of mine was raving about your honey dust?"

Tessa smiled. Her organic honey dust—a body powder made of honey that made women's skin very soft and that was also very delicious to lick off—was one of her top-selling products.

"I have several new varieties," she said. "I'm sure I can find something that will work for both of you," she promised.

She had been working on a line of scents that were specifically for erotic stimulation, but many scents had arousing side effects.

Sage for boosting libido and quelling anxiety. Lavender to create a sense of comfort and safety, perhaps for lovers who were having rough times. Orange for joy and heightened sensitivity, and sandalwood, her favorite, to incite an air of earthy creativity, encouraging lovers to experiment and enjoy each other.

She was so excited about the new idea. Sex and scent were so closely aligned, more so than people imagined, but there were a lot of myths about scents, as well.

For instance, according to some studies, a woman's

sensitivity to musk scents was almost one thousand times more sensitive than a man's, being that much more arousing for women than for men, as previously thought. Hence, musk colognes for women didn't make much sense, depending on your sexual orientation.

Stopping for a moment, she closed her eyes, inhaling and remembering Jonas's scent. He didn't wear cologne, but he used a sandalwood soap that she had given him, and he had grudgingly admitted to liking it. She liked it, too. A lot.

She'd worn some scents including cinnamon and lavender around Jonas, the first known to arouse men and increase erections, the second providing comfort and an inviting aura.

People thought that sex happened in the brain, but the brain only processed all the things brought to it by other reaches of the body, like the nose or the mouth. Or the hands, the lips… and all the other parts she would like to share with Jonas.

Jonas had a very strong nose, and a firm, sensual mouth. She loved his hands. How he had closed his long fingers around her wrists earlier, even though he had been trying to stop her, still made a delicious shiver run down her spine.

"Miss?"

Tessa blinked, her cheeks warming as she realized she had completely lost track of the moment, and the two women were standing, gazing at her curiously.

"Oh, so sorry. I was thinking about which scents would be best for a bride on her honeymoon. Tell me a little more about your husband-to-be, his likes and dislikes, and your relationship. We can go from there," Tessa said, pushing thoughts and worries about Jonas to the back of her mind as she listened and focused on her work.

There was no point in torturing herself with thoughts of him—that was clear from how he'd walked away earlier, rebuffing her concern.

An hour passed, and before she knew it, she was hustling the two women back out the door to the cab she had called for them. It was normally still light outside, but the storm had made it like night. The winds were picking up, the rain coming down harder.

She flipped the sign to Closed and stared out at the wind-whipped rain, wrapping her arms around herself and holding on as a roll of thunder made a ripping sound that had her hugging tight.

She hated storms because when she was a kid, lightning had hit their house outside her bedroom and had started a small fire. It wasn't a major incident, the fire was put out before it became serious, but all she could remember was being shaken from a sound sleep by the crash of noise and blinding light, being hustled from her bed and then the sirens. Although lightning had started the fire, it was the thunder that always bothered her more.

She wished it was Jonas's arms she had around her, but that didn't look as if it was going to happen. When he was around, she hadn't feared anything. He made her feel safe. But he wasn't here, and he wouldn't be. She would be riding this one out alone.

The best solution was work, to keep busy. It was her usual solution to disappointment and heartache.

Maybe she could make some new scents—rosewood, jasmine and lavender for healing a broken heart. Though right now, as her mind rolled over all that had happened, she knew it would take a lot more than aromatherapy to make her feel better.

But it was a beginning.

3

JONAS FOCUSED AS he ran his fingers along the edge of the window frame where he used duct tape to attach plastic sheeting to the edge. His entire right side was soaked from the rain coming in while he worked, and the wind kept pushing the plastic around, but he managed, proving to himself that he wasn't entirely useless.

A few minutes after they had gotten back to their offices, Garrett went to help a friend whose house was having some serious flooding in her basement.

Jonas smiled to himself. Melissa, the friend in question, was a particularly pretty friend who had been making no bones about her interest in Garrett. Jonas wondered how serious the flooding problem was, or if Garrett was going to have a little fun during the storm.

Good for him, if so. His brother deserved some of that particular variety of fun.

Ever the responsible one, Garrett had insisted Jonas

come along with him, but Jonas had made a point of wanting to stay at the office, telling Garrett to go. He said he wanted to listen to some of the most recent recordings of case files, and that he would call a taxi to get home. Garrett seemed happy about Jonas's apparent interest in work, and had grudgingly agreed but said he would keep his cell phone on.

Jonas didn't plan to interrupt him.

Jonas also wasn't exactly alone in the big old Victorian in West Philly that housed their offices, as well as a few other businesses, along with one apartment on the top floor. He'd heard sounds on the other side of the wall and assumed the insurance office that resided there was open if he needed anyone. He also had Irish to keep him company, though the big old tomcat who had adopted them the year before wasn't being much help. Irish was about six, they figured, and had some nicks and scars from his battles before he'd found his home. In that respect, he fit perfectly with the Berringers, who all had their own set of scars and histories.

Jonas knew Irish was really a lover more than a fighter, though. The big male cat had been caught soothing a sick kitten that lived next door, and wooing the pretty calico upstairs.

Right now, Jonas glanced down when he heard the cat's inquiring noise.

"I'm fine, Irish. Just getting this window taped up, bud."

As Jonas sat reviewing cases, a window at the back busted when a small branch had broken off a tree and fell through it.

Right now, Jonas was struggling to adjust the plastic sheeting to keep the rain out. He had asked Rhonda, the insurance company's secretary, for help finding tape and plastic down in the basement all three businesses shared. She'd been on her way out, but offered to help, in the neighborly spirit of most Philadelphians.

Jonas had heard her saying something about "the kids being all right" on the phone when he had walked into the office, and told her to go, he was fine. Which he was. Mostly.

He'd cut himself once, a minor injury, and had a few bruises from getting up and down on a chair to reach the top of the window, but he'd gotten the job done. He took an odd amount of satisfaction from that fact. It was good to do something, to be competent in spite of his blindness.

When his phone rang, he frowned. He hated not being able to see the caller ID for who was calling, but just answered, since it was his personal line.

"Jonas."

"Jonas, I was hoping you'd be there," Senator Rose's voice boomed across the line.

For the second time that day, Jonas was surprised by one of the Rose family. Not in a good way. He hadn't talked to the senator since his accident, and had no idea why he'd be calling now.

"Hello, sir. Are you back in the U.S.?" he asked, trying to sound neutral. The guy had a lot of nerve, threatening Jonas's family business, and then calling out of the blue, sounding as if nothing was wrong.

"No, no. In Italy, now, but I'm heading home early and I'll be back tomorrow. Has your sight returned yet?"

Jonas paused, wondering at the question. The senator was calling to check on his health? This was getting stranger by the second.

"No, not yet I'm afraid."

"Sorry to hear that. I need your help with something, Jon," he said.

Jonas experienced a surge of excitement—had the senator decided to forgive and forget?

"I don't know how much help I can be with anything right now, sir. But I can refer one of my brothers—"

"It has to be you. I need you to keep an eye on Tessa for me until I get back."

Jonas paused, quite sure he hadn't heard right.

"I'm sorry?"

"Tessa. There's a problem in my office. I can't say what it is yet. It doesn't have anything to do with Tessa directly, but I'd feel better knowing she wasn't alone for a day or so. Oh, and this needs to stay between us."

"You don't want her knowing she's under protection?" He'd done undercover guard duty before, but this time he wasn't sure that would work, or that he even wanted to do it.

"That would be best. You know how she hates my interference in her life. It's only until I get back. Then things will be straightened out."

"Sir, not to put too fine a point on it, but I'm blind. I can't see how—"

"Jonas, it's true I was less than happy to find out that you were messing around with my daughter. It could have cost both of you your lives," Rose said. "I know she can be a handful, and she likes nothing more than to take a shot at her old man now and then. But you two fooling around plays in our favor now. If anyone has a chance of staying close to her and not raising her suspicions, it's you. Blind or not, you're probably twice as effective as anyone else. Just don't let her get to you this time."

In other words, keep it in your pants, son. Jonas heard the clear subtext.

"But, sir—"

"I need you to do this for me. Don't let me down, Jon."

The line went dead.

Muttering a string of curses, Jonas shook his head at the strange call. Tessa was not exactly his biggest fan right now. How could he insert himself into her life without her being suspicious after he'd thrown her out that morning?

The sound of something crashing outside the window made him spin back, and he teetered, falling to the floor, his foot still caught in the chair. The wind knocked out of him, Jonas lay there for a moment, getting his bearings. He grunted as Irish landed on his chest and began licking his face, obviously concerned for him.

Standing, he winced at the twinge in his ankle. Great. Just what he needed.

He made his way to the bathroom and rifled through everything seeking the first-aid kit he knew was there, and found the package of Ace bandages he sought, stripping his sock and shoe off. He could feel some minor swelling, but it wasn't bad.

Trying, unsuccessfully, to wrap his ankle, he gave up and sought out the familiar feel of the jar of painkillers they kept on hand in the cabinet. It was barely a sprain, more of a twist, and probably didn't even need wrapping, anyway.

However, it was clear he wasn't up to doing chores around the office, and he reached for his phone to call for a taxi so he could get home.

And then he paused, thinking about the call from James.

Like it or not—and he didn't—the request to babysit the boss's daughter for the next few days was his second chance, his way to make amends for his screwup the first time. If nothing else, he owed it to his brothers to try to make amends for nearly losing their biggest benefactor.

But it was more than that for him, and Jonas knew it. His mind went back to that night with Tessa, to kissing her, as it had almost every day since it had happened.

He could still remember every detail of holding her. Kissing her. Her taste. Her scent.

The wind hit the side of the house hard, the thunder deafening.

Tessa hated thunder.

Maybe she needed him. If James thought she was in trouble, or even that she just needed someone close by, he couldn't turn his back on that. But the senator was right—she'd never allow him to guard her. She had issued an invitation—one he hadn't intended to respond to, but now things had changed. It gave him an in—cold, sure—but he had a job to do, and this time he would do it right. She'd hate him afterward, but that might be better, anyway.

Before he could think about it too much, he hit the second number on his speed dial.

"Tessa?"

She was so quiet at first, he thought they might have dropped the connection.

"Jonas?"

"Yeah, I'm sorry to bother you, but…um, I…I need your help."

A SHORT WHILE LATER, Tessa was banging at the front door. "Jonas, are you there? Let me in, I'm getting soaked out here!"

Through the glass, she saw him limping slightly on his way to the door, which he opened. She hurried in, soaked to the skin. Rain dripped off her coat, puddling on the polished wood floors.

"The rain is coming down sideways out there," she said, glad to have an excuse to cover her nerves about showing up.

When she'd seen his number on her caller ID, she thought maybe he'd had a change of heart—that he wanted to take her up on her invitation from earlier.

When he'd said he needed her help, she'd been worried sick, imagining every terrible thing possible between her store and the office, but from what she could tell, he looked in one piece, more or less.

"I'm sorry to drag you out in this, but you were the only person I could reach," he said.

His last resort, she thought, her hopes dipping. This wasn't exactly what she'd counted on. "What happened?"

"I turned suddenly, and I think I sprained my ankle. I tried to take care of it myself, but couldn't. If you could help me out with that, and getting me home, I'd appreciate it."

"What's been going on here?"

"A tree limb broke the window. I managed to get it covered."

She walked to the edge of the room on her left, seeing leftover bits of broken glass.

"You're going to trip yourself up again."

"Why do you say that?"

"You're standing here with one bare foot and an Ace

bandage twisted around it and trailing behind you." She couldn't help but smile as she watched a big cat turn into a kitten as he followed the edge of the strap, chasing it. "Your cat seems to think it's great fun, though."

"Oh. Yeah, he would."

"How could your brothers leave you alone in this storm? You shouldn't have been climbing up on a chair—you could have hit your head."

"I'm not completely helpless, you know. I shouldn't have called you," he said stiffly.

Tessa took a breath, and swallowed her disappointment. He obviously hadn't wanted to ask for help, and in particular, he didn't like asking *her* for help. But he had, and she'd do what she had to do.

Still, she wished it was because he had actually wanted to see her. Her pride kept her from saying as much.

"I don't mind helping. Let me find someone to take care of the mess and fix up your ankle. Then I can make sure you get home safely."

She led him back to the bathroom and while she worked on his foot, he talked to Ken, their handyman. It gave her a chance to concentrate. Apparently the handyman lived close by and assured Jonas he would come over to take care of the window and everything else.

"This doesn't look too bad," she said, trying not to feel ridiculous that the sight of Jonas's naked foot was enough to make her pulse jump, but it was a very nice foot, by all estimations.

"Do you have any liniment?" she asked.

"Probably," he responded tightly. "I left the first-aid kit out on the desk." She pulled her hands back, and he seemed to relax a little. Did he not want her touching him even that much?

She got up and went to look, coming back a few minutes later. The cat purred around her feet and blinked up at her, clearly flirting.

"What's your cat's name?"

"Irish."

"Interesting."

"Fighting Irish, given his battle scars."

"Ah, that makes sense," she said, taking a break to scratch the cat behind the ears. At least one of the Berringer men liked her attentions, she thought.

"You're pretty good at this," he said.

"I dated an EMT once. I used to ride the ambulance with him when things were slow. I even thought about getting my certification," she said absently, focusing on the task as a way of resisting the urge to slide her hand up his muscled calf.

"Isn't that against the law?"

She snorted. "We weren't too worried about that back then. I wish I had known what happened. I have an organic eucalyptus oil that works wonders, and smells a lot better than this stuff." She hated the stench of the ointment she was applying. Running her hand over the back of his strong calf to steady his leg, a desire shot through her.

She was supposed to be attending an injury to a blind man, and even that had erotic overtones for her. How pathetic was that?

"You can probably manage your sock and shoe alone," she commented, "though I'm not sure the shoe will fit unless you unlace it."

"I have a pair of work boots over in the mudroom. Could you grab them for me?" he asked.

"Sure."

She made her way through the classic rooms of the

old Victorian, admiring the way they had remodeled and updated it without erasing its original character. The last time she'd been here had been to try to get someone to tell her what was happening with Jonas, how he was. Where he was.

The brothers had such a strong bond, seemed so loyal to each other that she found it surprising they would have left Jonas here all alone, dealing with the storm. Still, as she'd recalled earlier, he wasn't a guy who liked accepting help. She was just amazed he had called her instead of hobbling home on his own.

"Thanks," he said grudgingly as she handed him the boots.

"You're welcome," she responded in the same tone. "Let me see if I can just reinforce that plastic around the window to keep the rain out, and I'll call a cab."

"You don't have to do that. Ken will be here soon."

"It will only take a few minutes, and it will keep your floors from being ruined."

He nodded reluctantly, and resumed trying to get his boots on. So much for him wanting her around—he seemed happy to have any excuse to ignore her.

Tessa busied herself adding more tape to the plastic around the broken window. When the job was done, she phoned for a cab. It took three calls to find a company who had someone available.

"Our ride will be here in a bit. Things are getting rough out there," she said, jumping a little as a crack of thunder sounded as if it was splitting the world in two.

"You shouldn't have gone out in this," he said, sounding as if he regretted calling her. "I know you hate storms."

"Emergency Services has enough on their plate right

now, and I didn't mind. Don't worry, you'll be away from me soon enough," she couldn't stop herself from adding, hurt and disappointed that he was so obviously displeased by her presence.

She knew he believed the worst of her, but she didn't deserve it. She also knew from a lifetime of being a politician's daughter that once people's minds were made up about you, they rarely changed their views. When she had been bandaging Jonas's foot, it seemed as if he could barely stand her touch.

"Listen," he said, running a hand through his already wild hair. "I'm...grateful you came."

She didn't say anything, and the silence stretched between them.

"You're welcome," she said eventually, and was relieved to hear the honk of a cab outside. She didn't say anything else, either. What was there to say? She thought that she cared for Jonas; they definitely had chemistry, or so she thought. But she wasn't going to beg him to be with her. Still, it hurt.

"What about Irish?"

"He'll be okay. He doesn't do well being transported, and his food, water and bed are here."

"Okay. If you're sure he's okay."

"He has a cat door in the back if he needs to get out, but he usually just hunkers down at night."

"Let's go, then," she said, and he pulled back when she took his hand.

"Cripes, Jonas, relax. I'm just helping you out to the cab, not trying to come on to you," she said, gritting her teeth.

He blew out a breath, seeming as tense as she was. "It's not you, Tessa. I hate this, my situation and being led around like a poodle all the time," he admitted.

Her own aggravation softened. He was a protector, a man who wasn't used to being vulnerable. He stood in front of others who were. She put her own feelings aside, realizing how difficult this was for him. He let her lead him out through the maelstrom to the shelter of the cab.

"Hardly a poodle. More like a rottweiler with a nasty temper," she muttered under her breath as they climbed inside the cab, and thought she might have seen him smile, just a little.

TESSA ALMOST BOLTED from the cab by the time they reached her store. The silent tension between her and Jonas was intolerable.

"No more fares," the cabbie said, looking back at them as she started to get out, but Jonas didn't.

"My friend needs you to take him home," she said to the driver, who shook his head vehemently.

"No more fares," he repeated, shifting his light to Out of Service, and staring at Jonas, not that Jonas could notice.

"He says you have to get out here," she spoke to Jonas.

"Yeah, I got that." His tone was clipped and short. He was obviously not happy about that option, and she couldn't help feeling insulted.

It infuriated her, but she held her temper. "You can come into the store and wait for another taxi," she offered.

She'd call one herself, and make sure she told them to hurry, she thought testily, helping him from the taxi. He insisted on paying the fare, and she let him.

"Careful stepping up," she cautioned as they ascended to the shop, and he pulled his hand out of her grasp, taking the railing.

"I'm fine. I have this whole property memorized. It was part of my job," he said.

She made some faint response, noting that he did seem to move easily up her stairs and inside the door, as if he could see.

Why did it make her heart constrict in an uncomfortable way to think he knew her space so well? That he had committed something about her to memory? It didn't mean anything, she reminded herself. He'd said as much.

It was just a side effect of his job.

"I'll call another taxi," she said.

"Thanks."

Tessa was on her phone for several minutes, watching Jonas stalk around her shop like a caged tiger. She called one company, and then another, but no one could send a ride for at least an hour, if then.

The city was paralyzed by the storm. The taxis were starting to return to the garage for the night.

As she redialed, she watched Jonas lift one scented bar to his nose and turned his attention to her.

"This is new," he said, and she blinked in amazement.

He paid that much attention to her products? Most of the time he had acted as if he couldn't care less.

"Yes," she answered, while seeking another taxi service.

She didn't tell him what he had picked up was one of the soaps in her new Erotic Enhancements collection. That particular scent could intensify orgasm. Standing and watching him lift the soap to his nose, inhaling, made her skin warm. Her heart fluttered. From her brief experience in Jonas's arms, he wouldn't need any help giving intense orgasms.

"Tessa?" he interrupted her train of thought.

"Oh, what? Sorry," she responded, shaking her attention away from Jonas and sex. Even when he was being unpleasant, she couldn't stop picturing him naked.

"Any luck?"

"No, I'm sorry. We can keep trying, but the city is—"

She stopped as everything went dark around her. The store was suddenly pitch-black, no light outside or in.

"Oh no."

"What?" he asked sharply.

"Blackout. Everything just went dark. Really dark."

"Are you okay?" he asked.

"Um, yeah, but it looks like you might be stuck here for a while."

He was quiet, and she bit her lip. He certainly couldn't think she'd orchestrated *this*.

She stepped down from the register where the phone was, and started to make her way across the store, but couldn't find anything to focus on, and gasped in pain as she knocked into the corner of a display.

"Where are you? Are you okay?"

"Yeah, just having a lot harder time than you making my way around in the dark," she said grumpily. It seemed the tables had turned.

"You stay put, but keep talking. I'll find my way to you," he said, and she thought she heard a slight smile in his tone.

"This isn't funny."

"I know."

"I don't know what to talk about," she groused.

"Then sing something," he offered, sounding closer.

"I don't sing outside the shower," she said, and then, a second later, felt his hand on her arm.

"There you are," he said.

His strong fingers closing around her forearm reminded her of that morning, and memories swamped her.

She had been so frightened by his call, and then so relieved to find him with only a minor injury, that it had been easy to set desire aside. Well, mostly.

Not so now. Here, in the familiar setting of her store, where they had spent so much time together, it was harder to ignore her attraction to him, stupid as it might be. He obviously didn't feel the same way about her.

His breath warm and close to her cheek in the dark. She had a feeling it wouldn't take much to turn her face to his and lean in for a kiss.

"I guess we could go upstairs and wait it out. This can't last for too long. I could get us something to drink," she suggested.

"Thanks. I—" he started, and then stopped. Then started again. "I know this is awkward."

"It is. Here, I can use my cell phone to light the way," she said.

"Don't use your phone as a light. It'll kill the battery. I can get us there."

"Okay."

He grabbed her hand this time, his grip firm and warm, and she stayed close as he navigated perfectly to the stairs.

"You didn't change any of the displays," he commented as they climbed.

"I don't, typically. I want people to find things easily when they come back for a second or third visit," she said. "I have an area for new items, and they know where to find those, too."

"Makes sense."

She did use her phone as a light for a quick minute to insert her key into the lock and let them in, finding her apartment as well in total darkness. It felt comfortable talking about the store, something neutral.

"We're both pretty soaked from the rain," she said.

It had been coming down so hard even the short walks to and from the cab had been drenching. "My brother left some things here after his last visit. They should fit you well enough, if you'd like to change."

In spite of being soaking wet, the heat and humidity made the apartment muggy, and she felt a fine sheen of perspiration on her brow. Or maybe it was repressed arousal.

"I'd appreciate that," he said simply.

"Wait here. I'll get the clothes and some towels." She carefully walked into the guest bedroom and found the Levi's and a silky black T-shirt in a drawer where Tim had left them behind.

Her brother, a criminal defense lawyer in Chicago, wasn't quite as broad in the shoulders as Jonas, but they were about the same height and weight, she figured.

She shivered in anticipation, in spite of herself. The storm didn't seem to be letting up. Jonas might be here for the night.

Maybe… No.

There was no way she could sleep with him. He'd just think she was using him again, to get back at her father or for some blue-collar thrill, whatever. He'd memorized her home, her store, but didn't he get to know her better in those weeks when he'd been guarding her?

Apparently not.

Could she have been imagining the chemistry between them?

She thought back to their encounter in his apartment, earlier in the day. It felt ages ago. He wanted her—he just didn't *want* to want her.

Though in all honestly, she was partly to blame for what had happened to him. She wasn't guilty of the things he accused her of, but she did bear some responsibilty. She'd set her sights on him, flirting, tempting, and did whatever she could to break his control.

That had backfired big-time. She also hadn't believed in the threat that he was guarding her from, and he had ended up paying the price for that.

So maybe he had good reason to be angry with her. And maybe this was her chance to make amends.

"Well, I have the clothes, but as to skivvies, I don't have anything like that on hand, unless you would like to try on something of mine," she teased lightly as she entered the living room.

He did chuckle then, a gravelly, masculine sound that warmed her blood.

"Not necessary," he said, and that turned her tease into a groan as she thought about Jonas and nothing between her and him but the thin denim.

Her mouth went dry as she put the clothes in his hands, and then the towels.

She licked her lips, impossibly turned on by him being here, so close and about to take his clothes off.

"You can use the bathroom," she said quickly, turning back to her bedroom to change her own clothes, and promptly slamming her shin into the table leg.

"Are you okay?"

"Yeah. Though I feel stupid for not being able to

find my way around my own apartment in the dark," she admitted.

"It gets easier with practice. Maybe you should use your phone for light before you really hurt yourself."

She frowned, but did light her way back to her room as he disappeared into the bathroom with no trouble whatsoever.

Stripping out of her wet clothes, she dried off and applied some smoothing sage and lavender lotion to her skin, enjoying the calming scents. Her phone dimmed a bit, and she knew she was losing the charge, so tried to finish her ministrations in the dark.

Peering out the window as she was slipping on a pair of light capris and a tank, she couldn't see a thing. Rain hit the glass so hard that the entire view was obscured, and everything was pitch-black, including the streetlights.

She wasn't sure how she was going to make it through this night. She wanted Jonas, but he clearly had no such intentions toward her. They were stuck together, and she'd make the best of it, but she ached inside and wished things could be different.

Making her way back out to the main room, she did as he instructed and walked slowly forward, until she caught the edge of the flip-flop she wore on the throw rug, pitching forward and landing with a thud on the hardwood floor.

A lamp fell from the table beside her and she cursed loudly. That was her favorite lamp, a one-of-a-kind that she had handmade by a glassblower in New York.

"Are you okay? Where are you?" Jonas called, emerging from the bathroom.

"Yeah, I just stumbled over the rug, and I think I broke a lamp."

"Don't move, you could cut yourself on broken glass."

The next thing she knew, he was there, his hands finding her in the dark.

The scent of sweet-smelling lavender and sage lotion on her skin rose between them as he helped her up and over to the sofa. As he sat down with her, he didn't let go.

She'd dabbed some patchouli oil on her pulse points earlier in the day. The sweet, earthy scent was traditionally one used in erotic ceremony, and connected historically to sensual practice. Right now, combined with the humidity in the room and Jonas's manly scent, it was a heady mix.

Or maybe it was the way one of his hands lingered on her back, and the other on her wrist. The storm raged outside, but Tessa hardly noticed.

"I shouldn't be here," he said.

"And yet here you are."

She saw the green light in the tense posture of his body, as if he was using every muscle he had to hold himself back.

Time stopped. The world outside the window was invisible, everything was swallowed by the storm. It was only the two of them, here, alone, and suddenly nothing else mattered.

"Jonas," she whispered, but it was all he allowed her to say before his mouth was on hers, and they fell back to the soft cushions of the sofa, forgetting everything else.

4

JONAS KNEW HE was playing a dangerous game, but when he had Tessa in his arms, her scent intoxicating him, he couldn't stay away.

He didn't ask for this. If James hadn't called, he wouldn't even be here. But he was, and being this close to Tessa without touching her was proving impossible. It had been a mistake of grand proportions to accept this job from James, but it was too late now.

He wanted her more than he wanted his next breath, and in one move, he slipped off the thin tank she'd put on, and pressed her bare flesh to his. They both groaned as she twined her arms around his neck.

"You're not dressed," she said, rubbing her mouth against his collarbone.

"Not completely, no," he said, absorbing the sensation of her soft skin and pebbled nipples pressing against his chest, almost making him think he was dreaming again. "I was interrupted by you wrecking your apartment."

"Good timing on my part, then," she said, offering

her mouth to him. His hands drifted up and wove themselves into her hair, but alarms went off in his head.

What did she mean? Did she fall on purpose? Was
Tessa playing games again?

He deepened the kiss, realizing he didn't care.

"You feel good," he said, though it was a radical
understatement.

"You, too," she whispered.

The kiss went on and on, and he pressed his erection
against her belly with a groan. He ran his hands and
lips over her everywhere, committing every curve and
shallow of her form to memory. Rolling her nipples
between his fingers, he liked when she cried out, gasping in pleasure, and he did it again.

Her responses to him, at least, were real, and that's
all that mattered to him right then.

Jonas gently pushed her breasts together and sucked
in both tender nubs at once, feeling her entire body
tremble under his. He'd always been one to enjoy sex
with the lights on, but his blindness made everything
more intense, and this was no exception.

She ran her hands down his chest, unzipping his
jeans. He sucked in a sharp breath when her hand closed
around him, stroking lightly, running her thumb over
the broad crown of his cock.

"You're killing me, Tessa," he managed to choke
out.

"I haven't even started. There are so many things
I've thought about doing to you," she said on a whisper,
sliding downward so that she could taste him, taking
his length into her mouth. Jonas took a deep breath then
released it, letting her do whatever she wanted.

He set his hand gently on the back of her head, holding her there for a long moment as she drew on him.

Not sure he'd last much longer, he pulled her back up against him and, quickly, silently, slid the bottoms she wore off, and then the slight, silky panties, as well. He lay over her, his shoulders nudging at the insides of her knees.

Oh, yeah, his body hummed.

Tracing a line down from her navel to the slick, hot flesh of her sex, he spread her wider, and only wished he could see. She arched, wanting more, quivering.

He flicked his tongue lightly against her clit. He relished the hot, womanly taste and abandoned the light touch to go deeper, rolling his tongue around her, parting her folds and seeking the ways to make her cry out. He had no idea how long he stayed there, the intimate kiss pleasing and arousing him as much as it seemed to please and arouse her.

She bucked her hips against him, but he held her in place, one climax triggering another until she was left spent and panting beneath him.

"Jonas," she said his name on a breath, the satisfaction evident in her voice.

Masculine pride suffused him, inciting the urge to take her and please her even more deeply. For the first time in weeks, he didn't feel at a disadvantage. He moved up, he planted his hands on either side of her shoulders, holding back.

"I don't have protection, sweetheart," he said. "Do you have anything here?"

She paused and then moaned one of frustration.

"No, and I don't take birth control. I'm healthy, but I don't want to risk other consequences."

He agreed, and backed away, though his body tensed in objection. So close. Like his dream coming true, much to his frustration, except that she'd stayed with him this time.

Tessa pushed up, her arm linking around his neck, pulling him in for a kiss.

"There's a twenty-four-hour drugstore two blocks down. I'll go. It will just take five minutes," she said, already scrambling up to grab her clothes.

"Careful where you step," he warned, remembering the broken glass. "You can't go out in this storm," he added, and she chuckled, a low, sexy sound he liked. A lot.

"Jonas, I would walk through fire to make this happen. A little rain is nothing."

As much as he agreed, he couldn't let her do it. He was here to keep her safe.

"It's dark out. There are fallen wires, looters, it's a blackout," he elaborated.

"I'm sure it will be—"

Her cell phone rang then, and then again.

"Are you going to answer that?" he asked.

He heard her grab the phone.

"Hello, Kate?" Tessa said, and there was clear concern in her tone as she turned away to talk.

The wind rattled the windows a bit. Jonas sat back, trying to breathe evenly, letting his body relax, if that was possible. He was hard and aching. It seemed he was doomed to never have Tessa.

Served him right, he supposed. He never should have taken this job in the first place, and since he did, he really had to try harder not to cave so easily to his desire. But when he was with Tessa, it was hard to think of anything else, especially when the world was so dark, and they were here all alone.

She came back to where he sat, done with her call.

He could sense the change in her mood, and his own heat waned.

"Everything all right?"

"Remember my friend Kate? The pharmacy has canceled deliveries tonight and she's almost out of insulin. She doesn't have anyone else. She's also blind, so can't go herself, and can't reach her neighbor. I have to go get the meds and take them to her. I shouldn't be too long. Maybe an hour. I can get our other…supplies, too."

"It's too risky, Tessa. There has to be some other way," he said. "Call 911."

"They won't consider it an emergency. She's fine now, she just needs another shot by bedtime. And you're not my bodyguard anymore, Jonas," she said, obviously bristling at his bossy tone. "You can't really tell me to stay or go."

Of course, she had no idea he was actually there to keep close, to keep an eye on her. Which meant he only had one choice.

"I don't think—" he started to object.

"Listen, I'm going. She needs me. If you want, you can come with me."

"How? There are no taxis."

"We'll take the trains."

"They may have shut down several routes in the power outage," he argued.

"I'm sure it will be fine. Even back in 2003, in the big East Coast blackout, only a few train routes were affected. It's probably our best chance."

He sighed. Tessa had her mind made up. "Where does Kate live?"

"Lena Street, in Germantown."

"Okay, we can take the subway north, and figure out how to go from there."

"That's how I've gone before," she agreed.

He didn't see that he had any other choice, though Jonas had a bad feeling about it. This was not a night to be out in the city.

Still, he admired her concern about the elderly woman. Jonas had promised James Rose that he would stick close by Tessa, and he planned to keep that promise. He wasn't sure how much help he could be to her, a blind man traversing in a city during a blackout, but he guessed he was about to find out.

Norfolk, Virginia

ELY BERRINGER CLICKED his phone off, shoving it in his pocket as he finished his beer in two deep swallows. He pushed his glass forward for a refill. The wind howled outside, but it didn't seem to bother the bar patrons, most of them from the nearby naval shipyards. They paid the flickering lights little mind as they watched a game on the big screen in the corner, probably having been through far worse out at sea.

Ely had finished his assignment, guarding a bank executive who had been receiving death threats for the last few weeks. The FBI had arrested the perpetrators, a group of thieves who had had significant success getting inside vaults by threatening the lives and families of the employees who had access.

Ely admired the single-mom bank exec who'd had enough spine to finally step up and contact law enforcement. Several others before her had caved to the threats, and one of those had been killed during the resulting heist. Berringer had been brought in on protective detail in collaboration with the feds. It was a first for their small company, and a big step forward.

Now it was over, but he was stuck in Norfolk for tonight, riding out the storm. The bar was a place he used to visit often. He didn't recognize anyone here now, but there was someone he was looking out for.

She was late tonight. Maybe the storm had her hunkered down elsewhere, but he hoped not. Human beings were tied to their rituals, and Chloe Roberts's had always been to come to this particular bar on a Thursday night for a drink before heading home.

He hadn't seen or spoken with her in three years, since she'd interviewed him upon his return from Afghanistan and his award of the Navy Cross. The interview had been a chore—Ely didn't care for publicizing his accomplishments—but the brass had insisted, said it would be good for recruitment.

The night following the interview, however, had been much more satisfying.

He'd hung out with Chloe for a few weeks, while he was in Norfolk, but realized too late that he'd read her all wrong. She came off as a modern, career-focused woman, the kind of woman you could spend a few nights or a few weeks with, but who had no expectations of more.

In truth, she came from a large family herself, he discovered, and she wanted the whole package: a husband, kids, the white-picket fence. He didn't realize that she had set her sights on him for the prize.

Ely hadn't made any promises, and they'd parted ways more or less amicably. More on his side, less on hers.

He straightened as he saw her come in, her trench coat soaked, her umbrella bent all to hell. She struggled with it for a few minutes before throwing it into the corner in frustration.

Looking up, her normally well-styled red hair was wild from the wind, and she froze as her eyes met his. He nodded in acknowledgment, indicating the open seat by his. She didn't move for a moment, looking unsure. A couple folks called out greetings, and she broke the stare, returning the hellos.

The removal of the traditional trench coat she always wore revealed the same bombshell body he'd enjoyed three years before. She hung her coat on the rack by the door and strolled over, her composure taking the place of her surprise at seeing him.

"Ely," she said with something that almost approached affection, leaning in to kiss his cheek before taking a seat. "What brings you here?" she asked.

She didn't need to order, the bartender delivered bourbon on the rocks for her without being asked. Ely knew it was top-of-the-line whiskey, and that on a normal evening she would nurse that one glass for two hours while poring over her notes.

It was the same way she made love, he remembered all too clearly. Slow, thorough and with the utmost attention to detail.

Some things really didn't change, much like the rise in his blood pressure, and below his beltline, at the sight of her generous breasts underneath the dark blue silk blouse she wore.

Maybe this was ill-advised, but he hadn't felt like spending tonight with a stranger, even if all they did was have a drink.

He was hoping for more.

"Just finished a job, and any port in a storm," he said, then winced at his poor choice of words. She didn't seem to take offense.

"It's a bad one out there, but not the worst I've seen,"

she said, holding her glass to full lips that needed no coloring. He'd always loved that she didn't wear lipstick. He hated the stuff. "So you're working with your brothers now?"

"Yeah, personal security. How'd you know?"

She smiled at him, her eyes sparkling. Stupid question. She was one of the best news reporters in Hampton Roads, and she knew a lot about everything, and everyone, between here and the District.

"I'd hoped you'd be here tonight," he said bluntly, meeting her bright blue eyes, and also appreciating the way her damp curls clung to her cheeks.

"Really?" she said, looking away. "Why's that?"

He smiled and took another sip from his beer, shaking his head. "Just finished a job that reminded me about how crazy stuff can be out there. I don't know. I guess I wanted to spend some time with a friend," he replied somewhat truthfully.

"Friends? Is that what we were?" Her tone was somehow humorous, skeptical and suspicious all at the same time.

"I hope so," he responded, and decided to cut to the heart of it. "When jobs are done, the intense ones, sometimes it's like…"

"Hitting a wall? Like go-go-go then full stop?" she supplied.

"Yeah," he said. He knew she'd understand. "You're on a constant adrenaline trip for weeks, not unlike combat in some ways. Then it just ends, and while that's good, I—"

"Have energy left to burn?" she asked.

"Something like that."

"And you thought you might burn some off with me?" she asked, her voice hardening, and she shook her head. "No, thanks, Ely. I'm not interested in being another one of your pit stops."

She stood, ignoring her drink on the bar, turning to leave.

Ely reached out, grabbing her arm gently, but firmly enough to stop her from walking away.

"Hey. It's not like that."

"That's not how I remember it."

"I know. I wasn't ready then. I was just back from Afghanistan, I hadn't even seen my family in more than two years and when I was in the hospital, I wasn't sure if I was going to see them again, period. I didn't know how to get back to normal, whatever that was. You helped. I'm sorry I left like I did. I never meant to hurt you. I just didn't know what I wanted."

"And I wanted too much," she added.

"Yeah."

Her stance softened a bit, and she looked back over her shoulder at him, but didn't pull her arm away.

"Looking for a second chance, Ely?"

Was he?

He'd been back in civilian life for three years. When he was in Kandahar, he hadn't had a chance to think about the future. When he'd gotten back, he couldn't stop thinking about the past. It had taken him a while to put it all behind him and accept that he even had a future, especially after he'd come close to being blown to bits.

Eventually, he'd looked around him, around his life, at his own family, and realized he wanted more.

Did he want more with Chloe? Is that really why he came here tonight? Hadn't he been thinking about it for days? Maybe longer? A second chance to find out seemed right.

"Yeah. Maybe, if you think we might have something worth taking a chance on," he said, letting his hand slide down her arm to find her hand.

She stood still for a minute, as if weighing her decision, and squeezed his hand, nodding.

"Let's get out of here," she said.

They walked out into the storm together, making their way to her car. When she opened the backseat door instead of the front, he paused, surprised, but then joined her, the storm surging around them as neither had any interest in waiting.

He hadn't planned on this, either, but he wasn't about to turn her down. Hunger took over, and he buried his face in the soft volume of her breasts. It all came rushing back, how sweet, how responsive she was.

She gasped as he pushed her blouse and bra aside, holding his head to her as he sucked a velvety nipple into his mouth, drawing on it as he laid her back on the seat, pulling the top off altogether. No one would see them at the back of the lot, through the fury of the storm.

She pulled at his clothes, too, obviously not interested in anything slow this time, and within seconds, they were both naked.

He covered himself without wasting any time and met her where she sought him, thrusting deep, feeling her clamp down around him, the two of them coming together within a few short, hot minutes.

"Oh, no," he panted, embarrassed and unable to believe he'd been so quick. "Sorry."

"For what?" she asked with a slow smile that had him hardening again.

Pulling her up with him, he sat so that she straddled his lap, still planted deeply over him. She ground her hips against him in a circular motion that had her dropping her head back, those marvelous breasts positioned where he could lick, nibble and suck his way to ecstasy as she rode him.

The rhythm picked up, and they were both mindless, as if having waited for each other all this time and not able to devour each other fast enough.

She looked down, framed his face with her hands, and kissed him so deeply that neither of them could breathe. His body bucked beneath her as she cried out, too. He bowed beneath her, jacking his hips upward in hard thrusts as he came with a fierceness that left him trembling.

They were both breathing heavily, held close against each other, wordless as everything calmed around them.

"You should know you're the first guy I've ever done in a backseat," she said with a smile. "But I knew as soon as I saw you that this was going to happen."

"Really?" he said, kissing her lovely, full bottom lip.

"Yep."

"My hotel isn't all that great. Your place?" he asked, hoping this wasn't the end of their night together.

"I'll drive," she agreed as she pulled her clothes back on and they moved to the front.

Ely could have cared less about the storm, watching her every second of the drive, reviewing everything he was going to do right this time. He hadn't planned on a second chance, but now that he had one, he wasn't going to blow it.

"So how did you get to be such good friends with Kate anyway?" Jonas asked as they ran into the train station, finally under cover, soaked through yet again.

"She came into the shop when it first opened, and I made some special items for her. She was always very lively and friendly, and she invited me and Lydia to lunch a few times," Tessa explained, getting their tickets and leading him to the platform.

"Then her husband died, and I knew that they didn't have children, or other family close by. Her diabetes was affecting her sight, and just this year she was declared legally blind."

Tessa peeked up to see Jonas's expression, which remained stoic as he listened.

"So, I started helping out, visiting her more, and it just became part of my life. I never knew my grandparents, at least not on my mother's side, and my father's parents, well, let's just say they preferred my brother," she said, laughing shortly.

"So Kate was like a foster grandparent for you?"

"Something like that, I guess, though I really consider her a friend. I like spending time with her, listening to her stories about her and her husband, and she plays a mean hand of canasta."

Jonas laughed, and she pulled back to look at him in surprise as they boarded their train.

"What?"

"Somehow I have a hard time picturing you sitting with a bunch of octogenarians playing cards on a Friday night."

"Well, it was usually Sunday afternoon, and I rarely won. Those ladies take no prisoners."

As they made their way through the passel of people vying for spots, she heard him chuckling.

She tucked herself inside the corner of the car at the end and held on to the railing. Jonas was so handsome when he laughed, she thought. He was handsome anyway, but when he smiled, he became wickedly so.

Tessa wondered if he was ticklish, eyeing the way the muscles in his side stretched and gathered as he reached to hold on to the rail, as well.

"It's nice to have lights for a few minutes," she commented about the train, changing the subject, and then realized he couldn't know if the lights were on one way or the other. "I mean, shoot, I'm sorry, Jonas, that was thoughtless—"

"It's not a big deal, Tessa. You can talk about the lights being on, the sun in the sky, the things you see... it doesn't bother me. I'm not that fragile."

She pursed her lips. "Well, maybe not, but that doesn't mean it's okay to rub it in. I can't imagine what it would be like not to see."

"It's...not fun," he agreed. "But it's also temporary."

"What do your doctors say? Did they tell you when?"

She had such a hard time thinking about Jonas being disabled in any way. Standing here with her now, he still looked undefeatable to her. She felt safe with him, regardless.

"Any time...things appear to be healing, but I just have to be patient," he said in a tone that told her that patient wasn't his strong suit.

Jonas was a man who took control, who called the shots. She knew this had to be maddening for him.

"I hope it's soon for you," she said, leaning in closer to plant a soft kiss on his cheek.

He frowned, and she wondered why. Did he regret what happened back at the apartment? Was he thinking she was still just messing with him?

"I hope the drugstore stays open," she said, needing to refocus. "I should make sure they know I'm coming. Kate has to have her injections or we will be calling emergency."

He nodded grimly while she pulled out her phone to call the pharmacy.

"They are open for a few more hours, so that's good," she said in relief.

"We'll get there, and it will be okay," he reassured her.

"Thanks. And thanks for coming with me. I know none of this was part of your night."

"True. If I weren't here with you, I'd either be limping around the office with a bandage still stuck to my pants, or home sitting in the dark, not that I would even know it," he joked, and she was so surprised she burst out laughing. A smile tugged at the corners of his lips.

"Why, Jonas, I've never known you to tell a joke," she said.

"There's a lot you don't know about me, Tessa." He winked, and she thought her knees might have trembled slightly.

Was Jonas *flirting* with her?

The thought made her heart race. There was a lot she didn't know about Jonas, but she looked up into his face as he peered, unseeing, around the crowded train car.

She looked forward to having the chance to find out.

5

JONAS WAS SURPRISED that the trains were packed. While some of the peripheral routes were closed down, the main lines were running. He supposed it made sense. The worst of the storm had hit around rush hour, and with the roads such a mess, the trains were many people's only option to get home.

He could feel the heat and proximity of all the bodies crowded around where he and Tessa were tucked into a corner of the packed subway car. They were soaked from their dash to the closest station, a few blocks away from the shop, even having used umbrellas. It didn't matter. Though he tried to make casual conversation, all he could think about was how close she was, and what had happened back at the apartment.

He shouldn't have given in, but when it came to Tessa, he seemed to have a difficult time saying no. This time, hopefully, their indiscretions would stay between them. Senator Rose had said there was no direct threat, that he just needed someone to stick close to Tessa for a few days.

Rose had also been fully aware that Tessa liked to yank his chain, and was clear on the fact that she'd used Jonas to do it. Luckily, it appeared he wasn't holding Jonas completely responsible for the last time, but Jonas reminded himself not to be so reckless this time, even though he was on fire for her.

She was also confusing the hell out of him. He had her tagged one way, self-indulgent, self-interested. He didn't trust her motivations, and he still didn't—not completely. But that didn't fit the profile of someone who had traveled across town in the rain to help him, and now was doing the same for an elderly friend. Was she just playing a role, being someone she thought would appeal to him?

The air in the train car was humid and moist, though the riders were good-natured and fairly loud, everyone sharing a storm story or visiting with the person they were crunched up against.

He was pressed up against Tessa from stem to stern, and acutely aware of every inch of her. They stood inside a corner area, where she was against the outside of the train. He used his body to shield her.

He was hard again from the close contact, and grateful that it was so crowded, so no one would notice. It had been difficult enough dreaming and thinking about her for weeks, but being this close—especially after being naked with her less than an hour ago—was undermining his promise to the senator.

Tessa's breath caressed his cheek. She'd edged in closer to him. He lifted a hand, finding her face and rubbing his thumb over her cheek, her skin dewy from the rain and humid air. The touch was to "see" her, to measure her expression, her level of tension, as much as it was to just have an excuse to touch her.

"You okay?"

"Yes, just a little anxious," she whispered against his ear. "And far too turned on, considering our current location," she added, shifting her hips against him so that she nestled his hardness in the soft crux of her thighs. He bit back a groan, not that it would have been heard in the busy din of the car.

He leaned in, telling himself he was just playing a part.

She had played him before, right? So turnaround was fair play, as long as he could walk away from the job at the end. Nuzzling her, he found the soft shell of her ear with his lips, and whispered, "Tease."

"Not a tease," she responded, turning her lips to his. "I'll make good later, I promise."

He swallowed hard, thinking that if he inadvertently rocked a few more times against her as the train took corners and bumps, he wasn't going to last until later. He was so ready to come he had to do mental exercises to avoid it.

"What are you thinking about?" she asked. "You look so focused."

"Baseball stats," he said flatly.

She paused, then laughed against his cheek.

"You mean, like getting to third base, or sliding into home?" she asked suggestively.

He felt the vibration of her chest against his as she chuckled, and he had to smile, too. It felt good—better than good—to be so turned on, to be laughing.

To be with Tessa.

"Yeah, something like that."

He was actually enjoying himself. In spite of his wet

clothes and achingly hard cock, he felt more alive than he had in weeks. Suddenly, Tessa froze, and a collective gasp and sounds of unhappy surprise filled the car as it ground to a standstill, breaks screeching as everyone in the car lurched with the momentum of the train.

"What? What happened?" he asked.

"Power's out. It's pitch-black in here except for a few emergency lights," she said as people started grumbling and shouting around them.

A baby cried from the far end of the car, and the mood changed markedly as tension rose. A tremble worked its way through Tessa's body. He slipped his arms around her, holding her tighter against him.

"Stay next to me. It will be okay," he said against her hair.

"I can't see *anything*," she said in a hushed whisper, pressing even more tightly against him.

This wasn't good. Even friendly, good-natured people could be dangerous in a crowded, panicked situation. He noticed that a guy behind him was breathing too hard, starting to push against everyone around him.

"I have to let go of you for a minute, okay? Hug the wall, right behind you," he said to Tessa, turning to face the man while still protecting Tessa.

Reaching out, he found the man's arm and grabbed it before the flailing man hurt someone. The guy was shaking, starting to mutter in panic.

Jonas kept his voice casual. "Hey, buddy, you okay? Let's try to calm down."

The man pushed at him, but Jonas held firm.

"Let go of me! Who are you? Don't touch me! I have to get outta here, let me outta here," the guy started to shout, pushing at everyone near him. Jonas heard a woman gasp in pain, the man's other fist making contact, Jonas assumed.

People started shouting, and Jonas knew he had to do something before a potentially deadly scenario was set into motion. Sliding his arm up to the man's neck, he looped it around and felt for the slamming pulse at the side of the guy's throat. Tightening his grip as he slid his arm around front and pulled his forearm back, Jonas trapped the man in an armlock, trying to hold him still as he struggled to get free.

"Jonas? Jonas, what are you doing?" He heard Tessa's breathless question.

"Stay put, Tessa," he said loudly, fighting the man's huge bulk as he applied pressure.

"Sorry, man, but you need to chill for a few minutes until they get us out of here," he said, and increased the pressure until the man stopped shouting, the heavy weight of his form going slack.

Everything around them was eerily quiet.

"Someone help get this guy into a seat," Jonas ordered, propping the man up the best he could, the slack weight almost pulling him down. "He passed out."

"Yeah, with a little help, I bet," another guy said approvingly, and Jonas felt the weight lifted as others took him off Jonas's hands.

"Good job," someone shouted, and Jonas felt a pat on his shoulder.

"Thank you so much," someone else whispered in relief.

Slowly, conversation resumed and the tension resolved.

He turned back to Tessa, finding her hand with his and touching her face again to make sure she was okay.

He found that she was smiling slightly, and he ran a finger over her lower lip.

"That was pretty cool," she said.

The driver's voice over the intercom told them they would be stopped for about twenty minutes, and to please stay calm as people were working on getting them on their way again.

"He was a big guy—couldn't have him freaking out in here. People could get hurt."

"I know. And no one else here could have done what you did," she said, pressing a kiss into his neck. "Way to think on your feet, Berringer."

Jonas's heart beat hard in his chest, aware of her again, the two of them pressed tight.

"How dark is it in here, anyway?"

"Almost pitch-black, except for a few safety lights around the edges. I can barely see you, as close as we are," she said.

Jonas realized that this was the first time since he'd lost his sight that he didn't feel alone. Maybe because everyone around him was also blind, in a way, or maybe because he was here with Tessa.

"I hope they get us out of here soon. I don't think people will stand being crammed in together for long." She sounded nervous.

"I won't let anything happen to you."

"I know," she said softly.

He drew her to him, pressing his arousal close to her again.

"*That* certainly takes my mind off things," she said with a husky laugh.

"That was the idea." He heard the anxiety in her tone dissolve into a gasp as his hand covered her breast, her nipple beading under his palm.

Leaning in, he found and nuzzled the throbbing pulse at the base of her neck, loving how it sped up every time he tweaked or rolled the sensitive nub between his fingers.

Her hand was pressed against the front of his pants, rubbing along the length of him. He shuddered at the touch, pressing in, biting the lobe of her ear a little more sharply before covering her lips in a hot kiss.

"Good thing no one can see," he whispered.

"Yeah," she agreed.

He maneuvered them more tightly into the corner, the people behind him caught up in their own conversations. Some guys had started singing, and others were laughing. More than enough noise to cover their own activities.

All he was aware of was Tessa's scent, the honeysweet taste of her kiss, and her nimble, satiny fingers as they slid his zipper down and then wrapped around his shaft.

"Tessa, I don't think—"

"Yes, don't think. Thinking is way overrated," she murmured against his lips as she slid her tongue against his in a thrusting rhythm that matched the way she was stroking him.

Jonas was normally a highly private person, and he couldn't believe he was letting her do this in a crowded subway car, but he was also too far gone to care. Too needy, too close to the edge.

If the lights came on, if anyone noticed, he thought, trying to find some way to stay in control. But that offered another surprise—the idea of being discovered increased the urgency and turned him on even more.

Her hands and lips were so soft, her grip just right, and his mind spun with the need to let go even as he still tried to resist. Creature of habit. As much as he wanted her, wanted this, he didn't want to give in.

"Let go, Jonas," Tessa whispered in his ear, her other hand sliding up inside his shirt and playing with a nipple, making him shudder and rock slightly into her hand.

"Yeah, like that," she encouraged.

When she slipped her hand down to caress his sac as she continued to stroke, Jonas sucked in a sharp breath, coming hard and fast with an intensity that made him bite down to keep from shouting her name out loud.

Pressing her back against the wall, the release shook him from head to toe, and he all but collapsed against her as she withdrew her hand. He caught his breath as he sensed her fumbling in her purse for something as he zipped up.

It wasn't the way he wanted to come with her, but it had been pretty fantastic, he thought, trying to get his composure back.

They righted themselves in the nick of time, as luck would have it; seconds later a cheer went up as the train rolled forward.

"The lights are on?" he asked, his voice still rough.

"Yeah," she said softly. "Thanks for distracting me."

He smiled. "I think I should be thanking *you*."

Her kiss at the corner of his lips had the heat building again, and he knew he would do what he had to to keep Tessa safe. Whatever game she was playing, he was more than willing to join in. James Rose had put him in this situation, and Jonas didn't care if the senator spontaneously combusted from finding out what he and Tessa were doing. It would be worth it.

Let her have her fill, and tell anyone she wanted. He'd deal with that later. Jonas wanted nothing more than to get her home, where he planned to drive them both to distraction for the rest of the night.

TESSA'S HANDS WERE shaking, along with her knees and probably everything in between as the others exited the subway car. Anxiety wasn't the cause; she was still so aroused from sharing close quarters with Jonas, feeling his heat, his passion—his *need*—that she hadn't been able to think of anything else but him.

The way he'd leaned into her, giving himself over to her when she'd touched him in the car had been sexier than anything she'd experienced, ever. He was surprising her time and time again. And confusing her.

He didn't trust her, but he did want her. He was angry with her, but protective of her. Would the real Jonas Berringer please stand up?

She was so glad that she had him with her in the dark confines of the car—especially when things had gotten tense with the blackout. The way he had taken control of the situation and kept her, and everyone, safe, had triggered a well of emotion that touched her deeply. He was an extraordinary man, though she knew he didn't think of himself that way.

She suspected a large part of his annoyance with her was because he liked her father. She could see it when he'd mentioned the senator, and how much her father had helped their personal security business. She also knew her father wasn't pleased about how things had ended, but Tessa hadn't been seducing Jonas to tick off her father.

She'd prefer that he knew nothing about her sex life, with Jonas or anyone else, frankly, but the senator made her life his business far too often. It rankled her to think that Jonas blamed her for her father's negative reaction, but there was nothing she could do but just try to show him she wasn't like that. That she genuinely cared for him and was attracted to him.

This was her second chance, and she wasn't going to blow it. Her father was out of the country and couldn't interfere.

Hopefully, she and Jonas could get to know each other well enough that her father wouldn't be able to butt his nose in again. Still, she was taking a risk. Jonas was clearly willing to think the worst of her. She had no guarantee that he wasn't just scratching an itch and would disappear in the morning.

Jonas obviously desired her, and he had said he would keep her safe—but did that include her heart? Though the sex was incredible, no matter what happened this night, she knew it wouldn't be enough.

So many emotions were scrambling around inside, she hardly knew what to do with them, especially as reality returned. They stayed in the car with the man Jonas had in effect apprehended. She knew they couldn't leave him, and that there was an ambulance on its way, but they had less time to make it to Kate now, she thought, looking at her watch.

Thunder still rolled overhead, sounding far away outside the train station. The guy in the seat had come to and was groggy and apologizing. Jonas assured him he was fine, and the EMTs would check him out to make sure.

"Where are we?" he asked.

"They diverted us. We're at the Spring Garden station," she said, tension winding in her chest.

The trip had taken her in the opposite direction of where she wanted to go.

"We'll have to find aboveground transport. I heard them say they were shutting down the city train routes until the storm passed." Again, she thought of Kate, alone.

"They don't want to risk another stranding," he said, nodding grimly. "That could have been really bad."

"There's a crowd of people looking for taxis and a line at the buses, so that could take forever," she warned. "Maybe I should try the car rentals."

Just then, a tall, black-haired woman and another man stepped onto the train, and Tessa saw EMTs filing in not far behind them.

Tessa could tell from her posture and stride that the woman was someone in a position of authority. The badge on her belt, revealed as she put a hand on her hip, cleared that up quickly. Philadelphia P.D.

Her green eyes lit with pleasure on Jonas, and then with curiosity on Tessa.

"Jonas! You're the guy who prevented a riot on the train car? I should have known," she said with a wide grin.

"That would be me."

"Well, that just made my job a whole lot easier."

Jonas smiled widely, and a twinge of jealousy grabbed at Tessa. He had never smiled like that for her, so openly. How well did these two know each other?

"Rachel," he said warmly, and accepted the woman's brief hug as EMTs boarded and took the man out with them.

Tessa stood, too, holding out her hand, meeting the woman's eyes. "Hi, I'm Tessa Rose."

The green eyes narrowed as the woman's head tilted

slightly to the side. "Detective Rachel Pankewski. I know you. You're Senator Rose's daughter?" she asked.

"Yes, but more importantly, Jonas's…friend," Tessa said pleasantly, holding the woman's stare.

The detective smiled widely, looking at Jonas again, seeming even more amused.

"So what happened here?" she asked.

"He started to panic when the lights went out. He was big, and started hitting, pushing."

"Yeah, we have someone with a bruised eye where he clipped them."

"I got him in a choke hold and tried to talk him down, but he got really riled up," Jonas said. "I know it was risky, but it was getting bad in there."

Rachel nodded. "He'll be okay. He's still kind of groggy and doesn't know what happened exactly. We'll explain the situation to him, and as long as the EMTs clear him, there's no problem that I can see. He was a public danger to himself and others. We owe you one. We're all doing whatever we have to tonight. It's nuts. I had an assault close by, so I responded. I'll write it up and catch up with you over the next few days. Thanks for keeping this from turning into a real problem." Rachel smiled. "What are you two doing caught in this in the first place?"

"Tessa has an elderly friend in Germantown who needs some help, she's low on insulin. We were trying to get there, but with the stoppage on the tracks, they rerouted us here," he explained. "We're trying to figure out how to get the next leg."

"You'll be stuck here for a while, and the streets are a mess. I have to go, but first let me see what I can do." The detective quickly reached into her jacket for her phone.

Tessa noticed two other things: her gun in its holster and her wedding rings on a chain around her neck.

"Old flame?" she asked Jonas, her voice not as casual as she'd hoped it would be.

"Old friend. We were street cops together, not partners, but had the same shift and we made detective together. She's a good egg. And very, very married," he added with another twitch of his lips.

Tessa's cheeks burned. She knew she was making an idiot of herself over a man who didn't even necessarily like her very much, except for the explosive sexual chemistry they shared. She thought again about how he had rarely shared the easy humor or banter with her that he had with his *old friend,* and she realized it was something she wanted with him.

She craved the passion, and the explosive sex, but she was interested in the other stuff, too. The things that real relationships were made from. The shared intimacy of tiny details that all couples experienced in everyday life. Coffee in the morning, holding hands while watching television, finishing each other's sentences.

She had no idea if Jonas wanted more than sex with her, or with anyone, for that matter. It pinched at her to think that was all they had, and barely that, even.

The detective joined them again. "Well, there's no way for me to get a unit down here to take you…we're stretched beyond capacity, as you can imagine. There is one possibility for transport, if you are open to it," she said.

"Anything you can do would be wonderful," Tessa said appreciatively, trying to make up for her previous jealousy. "My friend needs her insulin within an hour or so."

"Well, we've recruited some help from mounted

details, and I have officers willing to take you where you need to go, if—"

"Horses?" Jonas said incredulously.

"Yep. Some of the local cowboys and a few of the state police are offering services to get where regular transport can't go. They can get you there with no stopping, unless the skies open up again."

"I love horses, no problem," said Tessa. "I learned to ride as a kid."

Jonas looked less sure.

"I don't know, Tessa, maybe you should go, and I can wait—"

"It will be fine, Jonas. Just trust in the universe. This could even be fun," she said.

"Fun. Right."

"Don't worry. The officer will ride, and all you have to do is hang on."

"Right," he said again, sounding less than convinced. "Well, let's go, then."

The detective led them out through a side exit, and Tessa smiled at the large, handsome quarter horse that stood with his rider under a roof that protected them from the rain, which had lightened considerably, she saw with relief.

The quarter horse belonged to the state cop, who stood next to a younger man, dressed in jeans and a T-shirt. Tessa recognized him as one of Philadelphia's native urban cowboys.

The city had developed a program to help inner-city youth avoid crime and learn to ride, caring for their horses and riding them around the city, as long as they stayed out of trouble and did well in school. The program had some ups and downs over the years, and had

had its share of controversies. Struggling to stay afloat in terms of funding, it still was active.

Tessa supported the program through her business, and knew her father did, as well—it was one of the few things they agreed on. It was a good idea, and she loved seeing the horses being ridden down a Philly side street in the evening, the cowboys appearing like some vision from the Old West. She also liked to think about the kids in the program getting a second chance.

"Ricardo? Officer Styles?" Rachel greeted them, and introduced herself, as well as Tessa and Jonas.

"You think you can deliver these two safely to Germantown? They have a friend in need," the detective explained. "Jonas is a former detective with the force. Tessa owns a store down on South."

Jonas spoke up upon hearing the younger man's voice. "Ricardo? Ricardo Nunez?" he asked.

"Detective Berringer," the young man said happily. "I remember you."

"Not a detective anymore, but I take it you're doing well?"

"Yes. Thanks to you," he said. "Detective Berringer introduced me to the stables when I was a kid. He got me out of a crack house during a raid when I was ten and got me into a good foster home," Ricardo explained to the rest.

"Ricardo is planning to go to the academy," Officer Styles interjected. "He wants to be in our Mounted Division."

Tessa saw the pleasure reflected in Jonas's expression.

"Ricardo, that's great," Jonas said. "I'm proud of you."

The young man crossed to Jonas, who held out his

hand for Ricardo to find, shaking it and pulling the young man in for a quick, manly chest bump.

Tessa's throat was a little tight with emotion as she looked on. There was so much about Jonas she didn't know, and she wanted to know it all.

A roll of thunder was dull in the distance, and they all glanced up at the night sky.

"We'd better go. We can get you there pretty quickly, but we have to keep the horses out of the worst of this," Styles added.

"Okay," Tessa said, looking at Jonas. "You ready?"

He blew out a breath, offering a sideways smile that made her heart skip. "Ready as I'll ever be."

"REMIND ME NEVER TO do that again," Jonas said, wincing as he stretched out his legs in front of the counter where Tessa was waiting for the pharmacist who was gathering Kate's supplies.

"Oh, it was fun!" she said, smiling and looking as if she really had enjoyed herself.

It had only been a twenty- or thirty-minute horse ride to the pharmacy, cutting cross-lots, but it had been a bit rough considering he didn't have anything but his jeans between him and the saddle.

He hadn't been too crazy about Tessa riding with the mounted officer, either. Officer Styles had been enjoying her company a little too much, from what he could tell of the way the guy flirted, encouraging her to "hold on."

At one point, they had galloped across the park, and he and Nunez had to catch up. Jonas wasn't sure, but he thought he overheard the guy asking Tessa out.

Regardless of his confused feelings about her, he didn't want anyone else touching her or flirting with her.

Jonas hadn't been jealous of anyone in a long time, and he'd almost forgotten what it was like to feel this possessive.

He also reminded himself that he had no ties to Tessa, and didn't want any. The sexual chemistry between them was combustible. They were willing adults sharing some mutual enjoyment, but that was it.

In the morning, they would have to accept that nothing had changed.

Liar, an inner voice accused.

"It was kind of exciting, don't you think?" Tessa asked, interrupting his thoughts and sounding more relaxed. Jonas knew she was relieved to be at the pharmacy, and they could walk the rest of the way to Kate's. Officer Styles was willing to take her as far as she wanted to go, as he'd made clear, but once Jonas was down off that steed, there was no way he was getting back up on it.

"Exciting. That's one word for it," Jonas said dryly, and felt her nudge him.

"You looked good up there. You should take up riding. I can toally see you in a cowboy hat and boots," she said, and he wasn't sure if she was teasing.

"Not likely." He shifted uncomfortably from one foot to the other, recalling the ride. "I do have a bike."

"A bicycle?"

"A motorcycle," he corrected. "An eighties Harley that I take out on the road when I'm off duty."

"Very sexy," she purred, sliding up close to him.

"So, did the Mountie ask you out?"

"Hold on," she said, kissing him lightly and avoiding the question. "They just called my number at the counter."

Jonas sighed in frustration. She wasn't making this

easier. He couldn't get a fix on her. She was sexy and alluring, flirtatious and open about it. He couldn't see what had gone on between her and the officer, but he knew that flirty laugh, and figured she'd had a good time. It confirmed his earlier suspicions about her.

She was also a concerned friend and a kind person. A passionate woman who didn't hide who she was.

If he was really honest, maybe he was as angry at himself as he was at her. No matter how much he could blame Tessa for getting him in a bind with her father, Jonas had been the one placed in a position of authority, sent to protect her. He was also the one who'd caved to temptation.

And still wanted to.

It wasn't the first time he'd made that mistake. His mind wandered back to his last year on the force. His unit had been working with the Bunko Squad to take down an underground gambling ring.

The bodies of several people associated with the ring had surfaced around town, and Homicide was called in, where Jonas had made detective two years before. When Bunko undercover officers had snagged an inside CI, a confidential informant, to serve as a witness, she'd been given to Homicide to watch while the undercover team closed in.

Jonas, the junior detective at the time, had been on protection detail at the safe house. He still remembered Irena Nadik. Young, lovely and lethal.

The lethal part he'd had no idea about. Jonas had believed she was a victim, and that was how she played it. Forced to comply with a ruthless crime boss's orders, she'd tearfully relayed a story about her father's murder by the men who held her now against her will, the constant threats to sell her into the sex trade when they were done with her.

Jonas had fallen for her, let her seduce him, and looked forward to when the case was closed and they could be together. He'd even thought of marriage. Maybe that was how he'd rationalized breaking the rules for love.

He'd had no idea she was playing him the whole time. Slept with him, got him to tell her things he shouldn't have.

On the night of the raid, she'd drugged him, and used his own phone to try to warn the ring. Luckily, his partner had shown up and caught her before she succeeded.

The ring was taken down, Irena was in jail for a good long time, but Jonas had messed up big-time. He was suspended during an investigation, but eventually cleared for duty with only a light reprimand on his record.

But Jonas knew the truth. He couldn't look the guys he worked with in the eye each day and expect them to trust him when he had messed up so seriously. For a woman.

He left the force the following year and joined the personal security business Garrett was launching. It had taken him a long time to trust his instincts again, and that's what bothered him the most. He didn't know what to think about Tessa.

It was easy to focus on the job.

The senator was out of the country, and he was given a light-duty assignment to keep her company, make sure she was okay. He had no idea what the senator's agenda was, or Tessa's, for that matter, but he could focus on the job. That he knew how to do.

"All set. Kate's house is about six blocks from here, though we had better hurry," Tessa said briskly, breaking into his brief foray into the past. "The storm is winding up again."

He didn't say anything, still caught up in dark thoughts, but let her take his hand.

"I picked up a few things for later," she said mischievously, putting a bag in his hand, where he felt the corner of what he assumed were several rather large boxes of condoms.

"You're overestimating my endurance," he said.

"I just thought we'd like some variety," she countered.

Feeling cornered, wanting what he couldn't, and shouldn't, have, but not knowing how to walk away, he just kept moving.

"Everything okay?" she asked, clearly picking up on his change in mood.

"Let's get to Kate's before the storm hits," he said shortly.

He couldn't let this go any further.

He had to walk away. He'd get her safely to her friend's, then back to her place, and try to finish this job without making things worse. The crunching sound of the bag of condoms he carried seemed to mock him.

The wind was picking up, and she linked her elbow in his, picking up the pace.

"Is this storm never going to stop?" Tessa said breathlessly as they hurried down the street.

She guided him flawlessly, alerting him to step down or up, holding him close with her elbow linked in his. "It's like some bad *Armageddon* movie out here," she joked.

The end of the world as we know it.

Jonas twisted his mouth sardonically at his own sense of melodrama.

"Tomorrow the sun will come out, and it will just be a memory," he said, unsure if he was talking completely about the storm.

She yipped as thunder cracked overhead, and jumped closer to him, moving faster.

Jonas stopped suddenly, wrenching her to a stop as well, the flash of light obliterating any of his previous thoughts.

The flash that he *saw.*

He pointed. "Was that lightning—over there, this direction," he asked while pointing, his voice urgent.

"I think so," Tessa said cautiously. "It's kind of all around us."

Then it happened again. A dim flash at the corner of his eye, and he whipped his head in that direction.

"There!"

Tessa sucked in a breath, realizing what he was saying.

"Oh, my God, Jonas, you saw it! You *saw* the lightning!"

She let out a whoop and flew into his arms as the thunder growled even more loudly above, following the lightning strike.

Jonas held her, but lifted his face into the rain, eager, urgently wanting to see another flash, needing more confirmation that he hadn't imagined it.

Tessa's arms were tight around his neck, and he wasn't sure if it was rain or tears he felt on her skin. In his excitement, he'd forgotten how afraid she was of the storm.

"I'm sorry. I just remembered you don't like

storms. I…can't believe I might have actually seen something."

"I don't care about the storm," she said. "I'm so happy for you."

Then she was kissing him as the rain came down harder and the wind picked up around them. He gathered her up close, returning the kiss with everything he had, jubilant in the moment.

Tessa's not Irena, he thought, and neither were his feelings for the two women at all similar.

Irena had been exotic, different and had appealed to him as a younger man who was easily fooled by beauty and charm.

Jonas wasn't as easy to fool anymore—was he?

He wasn't so sure he could walk away, in spite of his temporary resolve to do so. They parted, breathing heavily, as the rain came down harder.

Jonas wished more than anything that he could see her. Maybe if he could see her face, her expression, her eyes, he could know if she was being honest with him. If any of this was real.

Soon, he thought, another bright flash showing up in his field of vision.

"We have to go," he said.

They ran the rest of the way to the address where Kate lived, and Jonas was relieved to finally be under cover as the weather worsened. On the relative shelter of the porch, Tessa searched for her keys.

"Damn, I left Kate's keys at home," she blurted in frustration. "How could I have done that?"

Jonas's attention was split. His body felt electric, as if the storm was surging through him. He'd seen several more flashes on the way to the house, enough to cement his certainty that his vision had started to return.

One of the flashes had even been very bright, from a relatively close lightning strike that had scared the death out of Tessa, but thrilled him—both because he saw it and because it sent her into his arms.

He couldn't find any way around his dilemma. There was no way to counter the damage that Senator Rose could do to his family, but he would take every chance he had to taste, touch and experience Tessa while he could.

"Kate will love meeting you, but I warn you, she's a real pistol," Tessa said, pressing the doorbell.

"I'm looking forward to it," he said, nipping at her earlobe. "You're delicious, you know," he added.

"Behave," Tessa warned playfully as they stood outside Kate's door, and she pushed the buzzer one more time.

There was no answer.

"It's me, Kate. Tessa. I have your medicine," Tessa called through the door, knocking again as they saw someone pull back a curtain near the window.

"Who? I don't know you. Go away," the woman yelled through the door, sounding frightened.

"Kate, it's me, Tessa," Tessa said again. "I have your medicine." She tried to turn the doorknob, but it was no use.

"I don't take any medicine. You are here to rob me," the older woman claimed in a high-pitched voice.

"She must have miscalculated for her next dose," Tessa said worriedly. "Confusion and paranoia can be part of ketoacidosis. We have to get in there."

"Call 911," Jonas instructed. "Do you have anything small, like a bobby pin?"

"No—wait," Tessa said, clearly shaken. "I do, here,"

she said, shoving something into his hands, dialing her cell phone to call paramedics.

Jonas focused, finding the door lock. He hadn't done this in a number of years, and he'd never been great at it, but urgency fueled his movements.

He found that not being able to see actually increased his awareness of the mechanism of the lock. Not using his eyes, he could focus instead on the sense of movement or resistance offered by the pins, and almost as soon as Tessa hung up her call, he had the lock open.

"You are amazing," Tessa said, opening the door, only to find the chain and a chair propped up against it. Kate really did think they were there to rob her.

"Time for a little brute force, huh?" he guessed.

"I think so," she agreed, and they both put their shoulders to the door and shoved, breaking the chain and pushing the door inward.

"What do you think you're doing?" a voice bellowed behind them. "I have called 911!"

Tessa turned to see an older woman on the porch holding a broom up in the air as if to swat at them. She calmed as she squinted, focusing in.

"Tessa, is that you?"

"It is me, Betty. I'm so sorry to worry you, we have to get inside to help Kate—she's out of insulin."

"Oh, no," Betty said, dropping the broom and joining them, sizing up Jonas in the process.

"And you are…?" the older woman asked him.

"Friend of Tessa's."

"Do you have a name?"

"Jonas, ma'am."

"Do you knock doors in often?"

"Only for beautiful sounding women," he said with a smile, and Betty smiled back.

"Emergency is en route, but we have to keep her calm and give her an injection right away, if we can, the 911 operator instructed," Tessa said.

Jonas nodded. "I can try to hold her still if need be, while you do that."

"I'll help keep her calm. She might recognize me," Betty offered, and came in with them.

Kate was resistant but weak, and still very confused. Jonas felt terrible having to restrain her, even gently, but he spoke quietly in her ear, saying small, nonsensical things until Tessa had administered the shot of insulin. Kate seemed to relax against him moments later.

"She passed out," Tessa said, sounding panicked just as the sound of the EMT sirens could be heard out on the street.

"The EMTs will take good care of her," Jonas said just as patiently. "She'll be fine. You got here in time," he said to Tessa, putting his hand to her face and feeling hot tears.

He wanted to go to her, to hold her, but he was supporting the unconscious woman and couldn't move.

"You're very handsome, you know," Betty interjected, silencing him and making Tessa laugh as EMTs came in and took over for them.

"I hope she's going to be okay," Tessa said, holding Jonas's hand. "Will you excuse me for a moment? I need to use Kate's bathroom," she said to Jonas, and squeezed his hand before she walked away.

Jonas chatted with Betty and a few other neighbors who had come out to see what was going on while the EMTs prepped Kate for transport.

"Tessa is such a special girl," Betty said. "She's always so good to Kate, and even brought us homemade soup when my husband was sick last winter. She even cleaned house for me."

"Really?" Jonas asked.

"You're blind?" Betty asked curiously.

"Yep."

"Well, I can tell you that she's gorgeous, inside and out. I hope you appreciate that," Betty told him.

"I'm starting to," he said more to himself than to anyone else.

Jonas thought the older woman might ask about his intentions, next, but was glad when one of the other neighbors engaged Betty in conversation.

He knew Tessa was gorgeous. As for the rest, he was trying to match his earlier assumptions about her with everything else he was learning, and was coming up short. All he had to base his ideas of her on were media reports, her background check and her father's opinion.

But he had his own opinion, as well.

Could he have been wrong about her motives?

"Hey, what are you doing here, Jon?" Jonas heard a familiar voice ask.

"Brad?" he guessed, not sure he was identifying the voice right.

"Yeah, it's me, buddy. How are you?"

Brad was a firefighter/EMT that Berringer Security had helped out a while ago. Brad's sister had been bothered by an old boyfriend, and Chance had helped keep an eye on her and made it clear to the ex that he needed to go away for good.

"I heard you lost your eyesight. Tough break. Job go bad?"

Jonas decided to skip over that, and got to the heart

of it, hoping he could use this connection to their advantage.

"Yeah, something like that, but it's temporary. I think my vision will be back soon," he said. "Listen, we're kind of in a bad spot here. I was hoping we could ride along with you. My friend is this woman's caretaker, and is very concerned, but we don't have a vehicle."

"The blonde? She's your client?"

Jonas could hear the high five in Brad's tone.

"Yeah. She's mine," he said, maybe a little more possessively than he meant to. "I'd appreciate it, though I know it's not usually allowed."

"I can make it happen. It would be good for the patient to see someone she knows as she comes out of this, too," Brad said.

Jonas thanked him and returned to tell Tessa, who hugged him tight, much to the tittering approval of the older women looking on.

"Thank you, Jonas. Thank you so much for your help with Kate," she said, hugging him again. Her concern and her gratitude were so authentic, he felt like a total jerk for ever doubting her motives about anything, and doubly so for lying to her about why he was with her.

If Tessa knew that her father had ordered him to be with her right now, he had a feeling she wouldn't be as thrilled with him. But he was also under orders not to tell her. James was right, that if she knew, she would not only be upset, she would reject his protection, and he couldn't let that happen.

As they started following the EMTs out as they wheeled Kate along, Jonas heard his name called from behind. Betty, the woman who had thought he was handsome, met him as he turned around.

"Here, handsome, you forgot these," she said

conspiratorially, pushing the small bag he'd dropped out on the porch—the condoms—into his hand. "Being blind is no excuse for not being careful," she added.

He choked out a thanks, and felt his face turn hot as he turned back to Tessa, who was laughing. Hard.

"Jonas, if you could only see your face," she said, breathless with laughter.

He smiled, optimistic for the first time in a while. "Soon enough, I think. Soon enough."

6

TESSA WAS EXHAUSTED, happy, relieved, hopeful and worried all at the same time as she walked out of Kate's hospital room. Everything was fine, and after being treated, her friend had returned to being her old self in no time.

In fact, Kate had shooed them out of the room after properly interrogating Jonas as to his intentions, and receiving only stuttering replies. Tessa hadn't minded at all, since she was a little curious about Jonas's intentions, as well.

He seemed to go in and out of high and low moods all night, as if he was waging some internal struggle he couldn't tell her about. She assumed it had to do with his sight more than anything to do with her, but she hoped that maybe he was seeing that she wasn't the conniving manipulator that he thought she was.

That was the worrying part. Jonas had politely excused himself so that she could have a moment alone with Kate before they left. Kate had held her hand tight, looking somewhat worried herself.

"You love him, Tessa?"

The words had hit her like a straight-on lightning strike, and her first impulse was to deny it.

"I care about him. It's too soon for anything else, Kate."

"Oh, that's ridiculous. I knew I loved my Hank within five minutes of seeing him and knew that I'd marry him within ten."

"Jonas and I have had a rockier start. I'm not sure he even likes me that much."

"How on earth could you think that? The man is out in a terrible storm, at your side," Kate said. "Men don't do that for women they don't *like*."

Tessa sighed, and related the earlier conversation, and how Jonas believed that she had only wanted to use him against her father.

"You were a child when you did those crazy things," Kate objected. "It has nothing to do with the woman you are now."

"I hope he realizes that. I think there's more going on, though I'm not sure what it is."

Kate squeezed her hand. "Well, I think he has more feelings for you than he realizes, but only time will tell. A woman has to protect her heart."

"Thanks, though it might be a little late for that," Tessa said, feeling tears burning hot behind her eyes, but not wanting to upset Kate after her ordeal. "But I'm a big girl."

"And you deserve a good man. I hope he's smart enough to figure that out," Kate said.

"I hope so, too. You be well. I'll be back tomorrow to help you home," Tessa said.

"You get some rest. Betty offered to do the same. You focus on your young man and making things work. I'll be fine."

"Thank you, Kate. I'm so glad you're okay. You really scared me." Tessa hugged her and still planned to be there the next day.

It was what happened between now and then that had her in knots.

Jonas had waited outside the room, quiet and pensive. He didn't say a word as they turned to the elevator, but then were waylaid by one of Kate's nurses.

"Hey, I have something for you," she said, thrusting a pile of blue scrubs at them. "Kate asked. You guys are leaving puddles wherever you walk," the nurse said with a grin, "and you're going to get sick. There's an empty room at the end of the hall, with a bathroom. Feel free to go down there and get clean and dry before you head out."

Tessa was sure she'd just died and gone to heaven— her skin was clammy, and her hair was dripping down her back. She felt like a drowned rat and was, selfishly, kind of glad that Jonas couldn't see her.

She knew she looked like hell. Surgical scrubs weren't exactly fashionable, but they were soft, clean and dry, and she took Jonas's hand and headed for the room.

"This is awesome," she said, giddy with relief as she walked in and shut the door.

"I have to admit, it would be great to get out of these soggy jeans, and to wash the horse smell off," he admitted, stripping off his jacket.

The shower in the bath was only big enough for a single person, so much to Tessa's disappointment, they cleaned up quickly using what shampoo and soap were available. They weren't as nice as the things at her shop, but she felt a million times better when she emerged. The scrubs fit just right, and were so comfortable. She sat back on the bed and waited for Jonas as he did the same.

Was this the end of their evening, or just the beginning? Had he changed his mind about wanting to be with her? A few minutes later, he emerged, dressed and smelling completely horse free. She had to admit, it was an improvement.

"You look like McDreamy," she said with a grin, and wondered if they dared commandeer the room any longer to make use of the bed.

Jonas smiled, but didn't go to her. Had he changed his mind?

"We'd better be on our way," he suggested, and she agreed, trying to hide her disappointment as they made their way to the main entrance.

Awkward tension settled between them as they stood beneath the fluorescent hospital lights.

"Crazy night," she said, hating small talk, but unsure what else to say.

"Trains, taxis, horses and ambulances," he agreed with a short chuckle. "What next?"

Their answer came as they stepped out to the main entrance, and looked for their cab.

"Not here yet," Tessa said, feeling increasingly tense. "Things are so overwhelming tonight for everyone."

"It might take some time."

Were they still talking about the storm? she wondered.

He seemed preoccupied and distant, and she wasn't sure what to do.

A stretch limo pulled up and parked in front of them.

Tessa watched the driver get out, an older man clad in a long raincoat and hat, who held two huge umbrellas as he made his way to the main entrance.

Looking at her and then Jonas, he approached them with a smile. Tessa figured he was seeking shelter himself or thought they were his clients.

No such luck.

"Tessa Rose?"

She paused in surprise. "Yes, that's me."

"I'm your driver, Collins. This way, please," the driver said, and held the two umbrellas out to them.

"Wait, there's some mistake," she sputtered, and then halted. "Did Senator Rose send you?" she asked cautiously.

The driver seemed surprised. "No. I received a call from Ms. Masters to come pick you up here. At your service, miss," the driver said again, guiding a shocked Tessa to the passenger door, and then helping to guide Jonas to the other side.

Kate sent them a limo?

Only then did she note the name of the transport company embossed on the inside of the rich leather door.

Masters's Luxury Transport.

"Kate owns the limo service?" Tessa said in shock, catching Collins's smile in the rearview mirror.

"Yes, ma'am. It's a small company with only five vehicles, but we do a steady business. Her husband started it many years ago, and left the majority of it to her when he died, with a small share going to me, as well, for my retirement, but I enjoy the work. Hank Masters hired me twenty-five years ago. He was a good man."

Tessa sat back in the luxurious seat, shocked. She never would have guessed. Kate lived so conservatively, and even took the bus and train to get around town, at least as far as Tessa knew.

Collins leaned in, his arm on the door. "Kate told me what you did for her tonight. She tried to contact me earlier in the evening, to pick up her medicine for her, but I was in Baltimore dropping off a couple to their wedding and couldn't get back in time. Thank you, ma'am and sir," Collins said expressively, obviously very fond of his employer.

"I would do anything for Kate," Tessa said truthfully, taking Jonas's hand. "And thank goodness Jonas could get that door open," she said. "I could never have done it by myself."

"You let me know if you need anything," Collins said. "I am at your disposal for as long as you need me."

Kate was obviously trying to help her and Jonas along a little, Tessa guessed. A compartment opened on the other side, sliding out to reveal a champagne bar, strawberries and pretty, foil-wrapped chocolates.

"Some privacy, perhaps?" Collins asked with a twinkle in his eye.

Tessa, still stunned, nodded.

"Enjoy," was all Collins said as he closed the door and slid into the driver's seat, which seemed yards away from where they sat. A solid, and probably soundproof, barrier rose between them. A minute later, the car pulled smoothly away from the hospital.

The vehicle seemed to cut through the wind and rain like butter, the dark windows lit only now and then by a flash of lightning.

"I can't get over this," she said. "In all the time I've known Kate, she never said a word about owning a business."

"It sounds like it was her husband's venture, and maybe Collins runs it now," Jonas agreed.

"I'm so relieved. I always worry about her being comfortable, or paying her bills."

"People of their generation don't make an issue out of wealth like some do," Jonas said. "It's good to have friends who care about you. Kate obviously values that," he said.

"I do, too," Tessa responded, hoping he knew how much she meant it.

A buzzer sounded. Tessa pressed the button that lit up on the console.

"Yes?"

"I have your addresses, ma'am, but Ms. Masters wondered if you would like a late meal, since you may have missed dinner while getting to her apartment. There's no hurry."

"Now that you mention it, I am hungry," Tessa said. "And please call me Tessa. But we're not really dressed for dinner," she said. They looked like a couple of surgeons coming home from work.

The idea triggered a fun idea for role play—she would love to play doctor with Jonas, she thought mischievously, but then returned her attention to Collins.

"If you have any preference, let me know. I'm sure your attire won't be an issue."

An idea sparked immediately, and Tessa put down the divider, climbing forward to whisper something in Collins's ear. She knew the perfect place.

Putting the divider back, she eyed the champagne. "Okay then. I guess we're riding in style," she said to Jonas as she poured two glasses of champagne and went back to sit by his side, handing him one.

"I'm so glad it wasn't my dad who sent this car," she said honestly.

"Why?" Jonas asked, and she wasn't sure if she detected a note of suspicion in his tone.

"I don't like owing him anything, or having him monitor my movements. He says he doesn't, or that he's just trying to keep me safe, but I know old habits are hard to break."

"He's just looking out for you. Dads are usually protective of their daughters."

"Protective is one thing. Dad takes it to a whole other level."

"How so?" Jonas asked.

"When I was young, we were close," Tessa said, remembering.

Her father had been the sun, moon and stars back then. He'd taught her to ride a bike, played tea party with her and had sent her first flowers, delivered by a florist on her thirteenth birthday.

"But he confuses protection with control. I don't like to be controlled," she said, remembering less pleasant teenage years when her father had made her life miserable more than once. "As I got older, I realized he wanted me to be who he wanted, not who I am."

"Isn't that typical with teenagers and parents? My brothers and I gave my parents a few tough moments, as well. All teenagers rebel."

"It was more than that. I couldn't have a normal social life, even more so than what happens with other politicians' kids. He wanted to approve my friends, my activities, my boyfriends. It seemed like I only mattered so far as I was a reflection on him."

"I'm sure he didn't think that," Jonas said. "Your

father has always seemed to genuinely care for you. He's proud of you."

Tessa snorted. "That's the image he shows to everyone else. He was furious when I dropped out of college."

"Seems like most parents would be."

"Yeah, probably, but I was only studying law because he wanted me to. I'd gotten into soap-making as a hobby, but I loved it. I was good at it. I was selling soaps online and to classmates out of my dorm room," she said with a laugh.

"You couldn't do both?"

"I didn't want to. Maybe if he had let me do something more creative, more…me, I would have stuck it out, but I hated what I was doing, and I knew I wanted to open a shop. He thought that it was frivolous, the shop, the soap-making. He forbade me to do it. He tried to stop me, at first."

"How?"

"He blocked the business loans I applied for, and did anything else he could to thwart me," she said, remembering how ugly that had gotten.

A woman who had been buying her products for a while, who also happened to work in credit services, told Tessa why her bank loans weren't getting approval.

She'd been furious and felt betrayed by her father in the most hurtful way.

"He really did that?" Jonas said, sitting up, his blind gaze focused on her as she spoke.

She knew he only saw the facade her father provided, the solid politician who cared about country and family. The man who put up with a wayward daughter who was selfish and ungrateful. It was what everyone saw.

James believed his own press, and she figured he really thought he did the things he did for her own good.

"Yeah, he really did that, and more."

"Like?"

"Well, the worst offense, other than the store, was paying off a guy I was crazy about in college. He was in the music program, wanted to be a guitar player. We were so in love… and suddenly he received a paid scholarship to Juilliard."

"That's a huge break," Jonas said, frowning.

"Yeah. One that my father funded, I found out later. He would have had a heart attack if I had married a rock guitarist."

"Oh," Jonas said, frowning deeper. "So what happened with the store?"

"I proved to him that I can play hardball just as well as he can. I knew a city reporter, a guy who was dating a friend of mine, and I told Dad if he didn't get his nose out of my business, I would leak the story to the press, about how a city councilman, which was his job then, was using his clout with local banks to block small-business loans. If I went on record, it would have been a nasty political blow," she said. "And I had the paperwork to prove it."

"That sounds…bad."

"It was. He backed off and let the loan go through. It didn't matter. If he hadn't, I would have just used my trust fund left to me by my grandfather. He couldn't touch that, but I didn't want to use it if I didn't have to."

She sighed. "We didn't speak to or see each other for two years after that. Then my mom got sick, and when we were trying to be there for her, and after she was gone, it brought us together again. He had to admit

I was doing well, and things got better. He even came to the shop, and we have lunch now and then. But I'm always wary of him."

"I had no idea," Jonas said quietly.

"No one does. My exploits, as you know, were fairly well noted in the media. I know I was wrong to act out like I did back then, but I couldn't help it. He was smothering. He says it's all out of love, and I think he believes that sometimes, but it's hard for him to let me be who I am."

"You're probably more like him than you think," Jonas said.

Tessa drew back. "Why would you say that?"

"I'm sorry. It didn't come out how I meant it. Just that…you'd have to be a strong personality not to let someone like him, with his own strong presence, completely obliterate you."

She took a deep breath, and released it, relieved. "Yeah. I never thought about it that way, but I suppose that's probably why we came at each other so hard over the years."

Jonas was quiet then, his face pensive, and she watched him closely.

"What are you thinking about?"

He blinked, as if not realizing he had mentally wandered off.

"Oh, sorry. I just can't imagine growing up with all that pressure."

"Different families have different dynamics."

"Yeah."

She noticed he hadn't taken even one sip of his champagne. "You don't like your drink?"

"Not thirsty."

"Me, neither," she agreed, and set the glasses down.

She quickly stripped off her scrubs and returned to the seat, straddling his lap. His arm grazed her bare skin, his hand finding its way down her arm to her waist, hip and leg, his pulse slamming in the base of his throat.

"You're naked."

"You noticed."

She leaned in to kiss him. "I hope Collins takes the long way," she said, bringing both his hands up to cover her breasts.

"Where are we going?"

The way his voice lowered and caught ever so slightly as he massaged her made her happy. She wanted him to be affected by her.

"It's a surprise," she said.

He didn't say anything, and seemed to be holding his breath, as if deciding something.

That internal war again, whatever it was, she knew.

So she decided for him, leaning forward and kissing him until she had his complete attention. If he still thought she was seducing him for her own purposes, he was right.

Maybe he had the intentions wrong, but this was definitely selfish. She wanted him, and she knew he wanted her. She was willing to deal with any backlash later to have him now.

But he seemed to come around to her way of thinking rather easily, taking her into his arms and easing her down to her back. She stretched out on the sumptuous leather, and he followed, covering her with his own body.

She pushed his shirt up over his head, and he kicked his pants off. Then they were skin to skin, head to toe, and she almost purred when the strong, muscular legs wedged in between her thighs in a very erotic way. He didn't rush to get inside her, but lay there, covering her, touching her and whispering sweet things she'd never forget.

Tessa closed her eyes in the bliss of Jonas's body against her. As they settled into each other, nestled in the soft leather of the seat, Tessa had a sense of rightness she hadn't ever felt before. She knew she was meant to be with this man. She had the rest of the night to convince him of that.

JONAS WAS A GONER as soon as he'd realized Tessa was naked.

Though their discussion had created more questions than answers for him, at the moment he had had five feet seven inches of delectable, delicious woman spread out beneath him.

He sighed softly against the skin just below her ear.

"This is nice," she said breathlessly.

"*Nice* is a weak word," he said lightly, nipping her earlobe, then sucking on it, swirling his tongue around the delicate inner shell. "Awesome. Fantastic. Mind-bending," he offered, punctuating each word with a kiss, then a bite, then another kiss to soothe the sting.

Jonas was so hungry for her he didn't know where to start. His hands explored lower, sliding down the smooth lines of her back to cup her firm ass and pull her up against him. He groaned as his erection rubbed against a soft patch of curls and slick flesh.

Being so close with Tessa shook him to his core. He took his time, moving his shaft slowly along her sex, driving them both crazy. He was gratified when her nails dug into his back and she pushed up against him, seeking him, a wordless sigh and whole-body tremor releasing yet another wash of heat from her body.

She made the prettiest sounds, her body cradling his perfectly. Drawing a lush, erect nipple in between his lips, he let the sensations of touch and taste roll over him.

"I wish I could see you," he said, rising to find her lips for a kiss. "I've only ever touched you in the dark."

"You're right," she said softly. "I hadn't realized that. It will come back, Jonas." She moved against him. "And when it does, I'll still be here, if you want me to be."

Her words made him ache. He was starting to want that more than just about anything, and that was dangerous, he knew. What she'd told him about her father had explained a lot. Jonas had made a hell of a leap based on partial information.

And he was keeping a secret that would tear her from his arms, he knew.

"I guess until then touching and tasting every inch of you will have to suffice," he teased, injecting lightness into his voice, though his heart was heavy.

"I can live with that," she said, sliding her hand down his chest to his lower stomach, finally caressing his cock and making him suck in a sharp breath.

As she left fluttering kisses all over his face, neck and shoulders, he moved to accommodate her as she worked her way lower and took him into her mouth.

He dived his hands into her hair, enjoying the multitude of sensations her mouth was creating as she licked and sucked, her warm mouth and soft lips nearly driving him over the edge. Pulling her around, he slid his hand between her legs and found her soaked, hot. He slid a finger inside, then two, and loved how her moans made her mouth vibrate around his cock.

"Condom. Now," he demanded raggedly.

The next thing he heard was the ripping of the packet. He held his breath, waiting, hoping…and hissed out a sigh as she deftly covered him, kissing and teasing while she did.

Jonas eased her back on the seat, sliding his hand down to her ankle and pulling it up to rest against his shoulder.

"I've dreamed of this," he confessed.

"Me, too."

Turning his mouth to find the soft skin of her inner leg, he moved his fingers down to the crux of her body, seeking the hard, pebbled nub of her clit and stroking in slow, rhythmic motions.

Tessa's whole body twisted toward him on the seat as she sought more, writhing under his touch, her gasps and moans increasingly urgent.

"Jonas, please, I want you inside me when I come," she panted.

He pushed her a little more, turned on by her restraint, how she held back even as her body trembled with the effort.

When Jonas was sure she was as close to the edge as he was, he guided himself into her welcoming body, the very act drawing the breath out of him. She closed around him like a fist as he filled her with one, deep, purposeful thrust that made them both groan in ecstasy.

He'd never felt anything quite so perfect, he was sure of it. He paused, fighting the impulse to move, soaking up the sensation of her hot, inner muscles pulsing around his cock.

"Please, Jonas," she begged, arching up under him.

He granted her request, withdrawing slowly and then thrusting forward again, his hand caressing her calf as he tried to create the image of what she must look like in his mind's eye.

He nipped and kissed the flesh beneath her knee, opening her farther to his thrusts as he moved faster, letting need set the pace. She drove him on with hot, raw descriptions as she joined in, touching herself, telling him what she was feeling, what she wanted him to do to her.

He wanted to do all of it, over and over again.

He was sure he'd died and gone to heaven when he felt her hand down between them, her fingers circling the root of him as he thrust inside her.

"So. Good. Jonas," she moaned, alternating touching him and herself.

Pulling her other leg up over his other shoulder, Jonas pumped into her without restraint, all the pent-up desire, need and anticipation he had for this woman driving him.

The orgasm was like nothing he had ever experienced. Release created a splash of color behind his eyelids as it shook his body. He kept thrusting, and amazingly, when normally the sensation would start to fade, it was instead followed by a second wave of pleasure that had him gasping as she clenched him tight, her nails scraping his chest as she cried out her own release.

Finally the urgency eased and he lowered her legs, withdrawing from her body reluctantly and pulling her up against him. Jonas had never been what he would call a snuggly kind of guy, but he needed the contact as if to reassure himself that this was real, that Tessa was really here with him.

Her skin was damp with perspiration, which intensified the scents of soap and sex. Her body was pliant and he stroked her wherever he could touch.

"Keep that up," she said on a sigh, "and we'll be reaching for the box again soon."

"Sounds good to me," he said.

He sought her lips for another kiss, the heat actually growing again between them, when a buzzer sounded somewhere close. Collins's voice followed on the intercom.

"We're close to our destination, unless you'd like me to drive around more. If so, hit the intercom button twice."

Jonas and Tessa laughed at their driver's discretion in not asking for a verbal response.

"He drove all the way from Baltimore already tonight. I think we can get dressed and give the guy a break," Tessa said, extricating herself from Jonas's embrace, though slowly.

"We can," he agreed, but didn't let her go before he pulled her in for another heart-stopping, promising kiss.

The next few moments were filled with the sounds of them righting themselves, dressing and hoping they were presentable before they gave the okay to Collins.

The car stopped, and a door opened on Tessa's side. While making love to Tessa, Jonas hadn't even noticed that the pounding rain on the outside of the car had lightened to a drizzle. The winds had calmed and he heard thunder rolling gently off in the distance.

As Collins opened his door, Jonas looked skyward, though he couldn't see anything. The reflex to look was automatic, especially now that he had some hope that his vision was returning.

"It appears the worst of the storm has passed, sir," Collins confirmed. "But the blackout is quite wide-spread and has not been rectified."

"Where are we?" he asked.

"It's a restaurant called Noir," Tessa said.

"I've heard of it," Jonas said. "They serve meals in complete darkness. The waitstaff is blind, as is the owner," he said, unsure how he felt about that. "But how can they be open during a blackout?"

"A lot of the businesses have back-up generators, es-pecially restaurants, since they need to keep food cold," Tessa elaborated. "Though I imagine they might have a limited menu tonight."

"That makes sense."

He guessed Tessa was trying to make him feel more comfortable, which wasn't at all necessary. He'd be just as happy going back to her place and finding something to eat there—preferably naked.

She stepped up close to him, and he could still detect the scents of sex on her skin, his soap mixing with her flowery scent. It was so sensual, he didn't want anything to break the mood.

"I've heard such great things about it, I thought it would be…interesting," she said, sounding unsure. "One of the things about Noir is being able to understand what it's like to be blind. I want to understand how you're experiencing the world right now, Jonas, but if it bothers you, we can go somewhere else."

Taking his hand in hers, she absently rubbed her thumb over his knuckles, waiting for his answer.

"I've eaten all my meals in the dark for the last

month, but I'm still curious about the place," he said. "It'll be fun," he offered gamely.

They walked in and followed their server's instructions to follow the handrail along the wall of the dark hallway to the back dining room, where a private table had been reserved for them.

"You are two brave souls to venture out tonight. We had dozens of cancellations, understandably," the server said.

Jonas heard Tessa's surprised gasp, and felt her stop beside him.

"Tessa?"

"Sorry. There's not so much as a slant of light in here. It's so *black*...it feels like it swallows you," she said, and her fingers closed around his a little more tightly.

"We don't have to stay," he said.

"No, I'm fine. I was just thrown by how dark it is, stupid as that sounds, especially since we've spent all night in the dark."

"Not stupid at all," the server interrupted. "People often have that initial response to complete dark. Though you may turn off the lights at night, most places still have degrees of light twenty-four hours a day, whether from the moon, streetlights, night-lights, et cetera. So the experience of complete darkness can be quite startling," he explained kindly.

"You're right. I never thought about it that way," Tessa confessed, sounding more relaxed.

"But you learn to use your other senses, and you learn to trust the people around you. You'll see," he said, and led them to a table, seating them next to each other.

"Being in the dark can be a revelation. You start to know each other in a new way, to find out things even about people you thought you knew well."

As they settled into their seats, the waiter offered a short history of the restaurant.

"Dinners in total darkness started, as far as we know, as early as the nineteenth century. In the 1990s, Europeans began experimenting with dark dining, dark bars and similar events. The Paul Guinot Foundation, a French organization for the blind, came up with the idea of dinners in total darkness called Le gout du noir or 'Taste of darkness.'"

"That's fascinating," Tessa responded. "But how is the food prepared?"

Jonas admitted that he, too, had initially thought it was only a marketing angle, and had no idea of the history of the place.

"Our cooks are able to see, along with minimal other staff," the waiter assured them before asking if they had any questions. He also cautioned them to stay at their tables, to keep the area where he walked clear before he left.

"Are you sure you're okay?" Jonas asked, leaning in close to find her neck, nuzzling it.

He was concerned about how disoriented and fearful she'd sounded when they'd walked into the room, so he made sure he kept touching as they sat in the dark. Though it was not all for her benefit, he had to admit.

Now that he'd had her, he was even more needful to be with her again. Soon.

"I'm okay now. It's very…shocking. I walked into this room and it hit me how awful it must be to live in complete darkness all the time," she said.

He squeezed her hand. "Well, this has been a good reminder that I've spent a lot of time feeling sorry for myself when other people have spent every day without their sight and go on with their lives just fine."

"That wasn't my intention, not at all," she rushed to say, and he shushed her.

"I know it wasn't. But I think when I lost my sight, my first reaction was to feel like this was only happening to me. The waiter, and being here, reminded me otherwise," he said with a sigh, regretting his own attitude over the last month.

He, at least, had the return of his vision to look forward to. Others never would have that. It was humbling.

"I'm sure my brothers would confirm I've been a huge pain in the ass," he said with a smile, but then turned serious.

"I think you're being too hard on yourself," she chastised.

She leaned in, intending to kiss his cheek, but ended up kissing his shoulder instead, making them both laugh.

"Obviously my coordination in the dark needs some work," she said ruefully, finding his face with her hands and offering another kiss.

"You were doing just fine in the subway car," he said huskily as the door opened again, their waiter returning with drinks and appetizers.

"Maybe later we can find a blindfold," she said in a suggestive tone. "One thing is for sure, your other senses really do take over when you don't rely on your sight. Everything is so…intense."

Jonas agreed. If there was one word for what was happening between him and Tessa, it was *intense*.

7

1:00 a.m.

"Ohhh...that's wonderful," Tessa said with a sigh as Jonas found her lips with his fingers, letting her nibble a piece of the rich cheese that the waiter had delivered to their table. This had very possibly been the best meal of her life.

Though at first it was awkward, the waiter's prediction had come true: as each course was served, they became more proficient at handling their food using their other senses, and even trusted each other's coordination enough to feed each other.

Tessa knew that she trusted Jonas with her life. She had, literally, on several occasions. She hoped their experiences together were helping him to trust her more, too. He seemed to have relaxed toward her since their conversation in the car, and since making love.

A shiver ran over her skin. She couldn't wait to get him alone again.

Tessa absorbed the experience of dark eating full-on. This was definitely something she wanted to do again.

After she let go of her sense of disorientation and fear of the complete dark, she found she could manage more easily.

She wondered if Jonas would want to come back here after his sight returned. She wasn't sure how she would feel about that in his shoes.

What she was finding entertaining and enlightening might be a bad reminder of what he went through. There was still a huge difference between spending a few hours in the dark and being blind. She knew she could walk out of the room and have her sight back. Jonas, and others who had lost their vision, didn't have that luxury.

Though another part of her wondered if people who relied on their vision weren't the ones who missed out. Being in the dark demanded such focus that it enriched as much as it denied.

"So tell me something that you could only tell me in the dark," he said.

She paused. "I can't think of anything."

"Really? A secret that you never told, a fantasy that you are too shy to share in the light of day? Isn't that what blackouts, airplanes and dark restaurants are for?" he joked, but she knew he was serious, too.

Her heart beat a little faster at the idea, and the seductive tone of his voice.

"Maybe," she said, unsure.

"Tell me."

Tessa couldn't believe she was so nervous. She wasn't shy, in fact, she was often the one who initiated sex with her partners. But there was one thing…she had never told anyone. She didn't know if Jonas would be okay with it. What if he thought she was demented?

"The problem with sharing secrets in the dark is that

we have to go out into the light at some point," she said, thinking twice.

"Tell me, Tessa," he said again, stroking her hand with his thumb.

Sparks lit along her skin and she almost expected to see them light up in the dark.

"Okay. There is one fantasy I've often had…"

"Mmm-hmm." His hand was on her thigh, rubbing lightly there now, and she had a hard time focusing.

"I'd like to have someone watch me have sex."

His hand stopped. "What do you mean exactly?"

"I'd like to perform for a lover. You know, just have you, for instance, sit back and watch. Maybe I could use a vibrator, my hand or some other toys, but I'd love to feel free enough with someone to do that, to know that they could enjoy just staying back and watching me pleasure myself," she said, her voice catching. She was getting turned on just talking about it, but also felt embarrassed admitting it.

"I can't imagine anyone saying no to that," he said, his own voice a little rough.

"Men don't want to think women can find pleasure without them. It's a dent to their egos, I guess," she said.

"Not mine. I could do that. If you want, I want to do that," he said, his hand rubbing her leg again, moving higher. "When I have my eyes back, I mean. Just say the word."

She was incredibly turned on by sharing that with him, and by the prospect of being able to do it. But as he buried his face in her neck, she pushed him back.

"Your turn."

He took a breath. "Right. I don't suppose I can get

away with the standard guy fantasy of two women, right?"

She laughed. "I know you can be more creative than that."

"I don't know. I have always been a pretty traditional kind of guy in bed. What you did to me on the train… that was about as kinky as I have ever gotten."

"Seriously?"

"Yeah."

"So is there anything you've ever thought you'd like to do? You know, the thing you can only share in the dark?"

She put her hand on his thigh now, mimicking his motion on hers earlier.

"You are evil," he said.

"Tell me."

"Okay. I've never done it, but I think I'd like to try…"

Tessa realized she was actually holding her breath.

"Maybe being tied up," he said. "and tying up my partner in return."

"Bondage?"

"Yeah," he said softly. "I've never trusted anyone enough to allow myself to be completely at their whim. To let them do whatever they wanted to me. For them to be completely in control. No pain or anything like that… or maybe just a little," he said in a tone that tantalized her. "And hopefully they could trust me in the same way."

Tessa took a deep breath to try to slow down her speeding heart.

"I could so do that," she said, enjoying the image of Jonas bound to her bed. "I mean, if you ever thought, you know, if you wanted me to—"

She stopped, realizing she had dug her nails into his thigh. When she pulled her hand away, her fingers brushed his cock, hard and testing the looseness of the scrubs.

"I'll go find our waiter to see if he can bring a check," she said quickly.

He got up, too, and as she turned on her heel, she bumped into the chair and stumbled forward.

Amazingly, Jonas was there, his strong hands closing on her upper arms, steadying her and then pulling her in to hold her close.

"Hey, careful."

"Good catch," she said, linking her arms around his neck.

"Mmm," he said, kissing her.

"We all go through life stumbling around in the dark, Jonas, looking for something to grab on to that makes sense. You and I, we seem to keep bumping into each other. We fit."

He pulled her against him, fitting her to him tightly as he deepened the kiss. She didn't resist, letting him take his fill, and getting hers in return. But for all the desire and passion between them, she couldn't help but think there was something else Jonas hadn't told her. Some other secret that stayed between them in the dark.

ELY SNUCK THE KEYS out of Chloe's pocket as he pressed her against the doorjamb, her arms locked around his neck, their kisses even hungrier after their backseat encounter.

She was gorgeous, he thought, sliding the key effortlessly into the lock and opening the door without missing a beat, getting them inside where they could dispose of soaking-wet clothes and he could take his time with her.

"You have great hand-eye coordination," she said against his mouth.

"I was very motivated to get that door open and get us inside," he responded as he deftly undid the buttons on her wet blouse.

"I wasn't talking about opening the door," she rejoined, nibbling at his bottom lip, making him laugh and groan at the same time.

She tried the light switch on the wall, but apparently the power was still out.

He felt...*light*. For the first time in recent memory.

"I'm glad you stuck to your old habits," he said, thankful he'd gone to the bar and that she had walked in.

"Me, too," she whispered, lifting a hand to his face, running her fingers over the stubble of his jaw. "Let me get out of these clothes—"

"My thinking exactly," he interrupted.

She laughed, and he liked how it infused her entire expression with warmth. Her laugh reverberated through her entire body, the cool, distant reporter erased, a vibrant, passionate woman revealed.

He'd known there was magic between them before, but he'd been too raw then, too fresh from his return to be good for anyone. He hadn't been ready for more then, but he was now.

"How about we get dry, have a glass of wine...take our time," she said, leaning in to kiss him again. "No need to rush."

He nodded, sighing. "You're right. There's time," he agreed.

It was a luxury he was still getting used to. Time had

seemed to stop in Afghanistan, and since then, it was punctuated by the start and stop of various jobs where he'd experienced things that often made him acutely aware of how time often ran out.

He didn't want to waste any more of his.

They walked into her bedroom, and he watched as she moved around the room, lighting several candles set on dressers and tables. The warm light revealed ultrafeminine decor that he only vaguely remembered, taking in the thick, old-fashioned quilt of cream and roses, the ornate, Victorian lamps and lacy curtains. It spoke to the old-fashioned, traditional woman who lived beneath the image of the hardened career woman.

The space was so feminine it made him feel too big and cumbersome, like if he moved, he'd break something. Classic bull in a china shop. At the same time, he liked it very much. She was different than the other women he knew in a way that spoke to him.

"You're quiet," she said, stripping down to the black bra and panties that took his attention away from the room altogether.

She had an amazing body, all legs, curves and delectable soft spots he loved to explore and hadn't gotten nearly enough of. The soft, flickering candlelight completed the fantasy.

He grinned, shucking his shirt, liking the way she looked at him when he did so. "Just taking in the room, and you," he said, wiggling his eyebrows at her and making her laugh.

"You're different now," she said, watching him closely.

He shrugged. "Not really."

"You were so closed off back then. I know that interview was torture for you," she said.

"I was still adjusting. It's disorienting, being in the desert one day and back here the next, surrounded by people who all want something from you."

"You never said much, even during our night together."

He didn't remember that. He remembered touching her and losing himself in what she'd offered him. But now he realized how selfish he'd been.

"I'm sorry. I wasn't myself then. I should have walked away when you asked me back to your place, but—"

He'd needed the comfort, but more than that, something about her had beckoned him. Something about Chloe had given him what he needed, which was way more than sex, even though he didn't recognize it at the time.

"I'm glad you didn't. I only wish you hadn't walked away after," she said. "Are you going to walk away again now? Am I going to wake up in the morning to find you gone again?"

"No," he said simply, the word his promise.

"Okay," she said, accepting it.

She put on her robe, and then grabbed another one from the closet, handing it to him.

He took the garment, staring at it for a moment. It was definitely a guy's, and that bothered him for a second. He looked up to see her staring at him, one eyebrow arched.

"What? Did you think that I didn't sleep with anyone for three years, just waiting for you to come back?" she asked, smiling, though there was no barb in the question.

He took a breath. "No, not that. Hell, I didn't even really know I was looking for you again until tonight... or maybe I knew it all along, since I got down here in

Norfolk. I was reading your articles…you're still an amazing journalist," he said, and saw pleasure bloom in her expression. "An amazing woman."

"I kept track of you, too," she admitted, turning to the dresser and fussing with something, opening a drawer where she put some items, and closed it again. "I often thought of contacting you, but I don't go begging. Though you were the first man who made me consider it," she said, walking up close and sliding her hands over his chest.

"I don't imagine you were a saint either."

He frowned. No, he hadn't been a saint. There had been some women, several, in fact, but none that really mattered. None he ever saw again or sought out.

"Let's not talk about the past. It's done," he said. "The present—and the future—are much more promising."

"I like the sound of that," she agreed.

She seemed smaller here, more fragile and feminine, her hair undone and curling from the rain, falling down over her shoulders. He slid his hands through it, feeling possessive and lucky—why did he wait so long?

Her mouth was like velvet, and he let his robe drop to the floor as he dived the other hand into her hair, kissing her until she was trembling with need. Possessing her.

His, he thought.

"Ely," she said his name on a breath when he released her lips. He was sure he couldn't hear it enough, wanted to make her scream it.

Falling to his knees, he undid her robe, slid his hands up her legs, parting her slim, silky thighs. Parting the soft folds of her sex with his fingers, he tasted her lightly at first, but as she heated up, becoming slick, he lost himself in kissing her, sucking the hard, aroused pearl of her clit between his lips.

Chloe knew how to take charge—one of the things he loved about her—and her hands held his head, directing him, pressing and urging until he gave her everything she wanted, which he was more than happy to do.

She did scream his name when she came, and he didn't let it end there, making her crest one more time. She sagged against him as he stood and took her in his arms.

Her cheeks were flushed with satisfaction, her pupils dilated, mouth soft as he kissed her fully. He wanted her again, but also wanted to wait. He needed her to know that he could be there for her, not always satisfying his own needs, oblivious to others as he had been before, when he left her.

They had time. He'd make it up to her.

"How about that glass of wine?" he asked. "Maybe something to eat to go with it?"

She nodded against his shoulder.

"I have to wait for my knees to feel solid again," she said, gazing at him with eyes he thought he might like to see staring at him every morning. Eyes he might like to see on smaller versions of both of them.

Whoa, Marine, he cautioned himself. *Slow down a little there.*

But Ely had always led the charge, committed to the mission, focused on the target. He didn't see the point in second thoughts or delaying action.

"I can help with that," he said huskily, bending down and scooping her up, smiling at her gasp of surprise as she linked her hands around his neck and held on.

"Ely, this is hardly necessary," she said, laughing as he carried her out to the living room.

"But it is fun," he said, kissing her nose as he deposited her on the sofa.

"Matches?" he asked, noting more candles on the fireplace mantel.

"Up by the picture of my father," she directed, pointing.

He saw the picture, and grabbed the box of stick matches, lighting one, taking in the portrait.

"Navy officer," he observed, sliding her a glance. Her father was a highly decorated submariner.

"Yes. Retired now."

"You never mentioned him."

"You never asked."

It was true, he hadn't. Besides the interview, where she had focused on his life, they hadn't talked much at all.

He lit the candles, and then walked to the kitchen, telling her to stay put. He had a lot of making up to do.

Coming back with a tray of cheese, fruit and crackers and a bottle of wine, he joined her on the sofa.

"Well, now I am feeling very spoiled," she said, taking a glass of wine from him. "I could get used to that."

"All part of my evil plan," he agreed, taking some cheese and crackers, and settling back with his own glass.

"So where are your parents? Norfolk?" he asked, intent on learning as much as he could about her.

"The house is in Annapolis, but they aren't there much. My dad has his sailboat there, and they live on the water for most of the year, sailing to vacation spots. They fly back from wherever they are for holidays, and seem to be enjoying life."

"Sounds like the perfect retirement."

"I don't know that I'd want to spend that much time

on the water, but my mother loves it. And for so many years they were apart when he was at sea."

"Squid are a species unto their own," he said, shaking his head. "The idea of spending that much time under water gives me the heebies," he admitted.

"Seriously? I thought big tough Marines weren't afraid of anything?"

"I didn't say I was *afraid*," he corrected, puffing out his chest. "Just that I'm not particularly fond of the idea of being under several hundred feet of water."

"Ah, okay, I see the distinction," she said.

"Thank you."

She grinned and threw a grape at him, which he caught in his mouth.

"So what about your brothers? I was sorry to read about Garrett losing his wife—how tragic," she said, more serious.

"It was beyond tragic. We weren't sure he was going to make it through for a while," Ely said, still feeling punched in the chest when he thought about his older brother's loss. He'd liked Lainey a lot, too. It had been a loss for all of them.

"And Jonas, Chance? They're well? Married?"

"Chance is Chance. I don't think he'll ever settle down, or find a woman who can put up with his need to jump off high things every other day," he said, laughing. "But Jonas has been in tough shape."

Ely related the story of Jonas's protection detail, and about the loss of his sight.

"That's terrible!" Chloe commiserated. "But he'll get it back?"

"So they say. No word yet."

"And you said he's involved with Tessa Rose, James

Rose's daughter?" she asked in a tone that alerted Ely's radar.

"Well, it seemed that way, until he backed off big-time after the accident. But she keeps coming around. That's like one determined lady," he admitted. "Why?"

He liked Tessa, actually, and thought it was high time his older brother found a steady woman, but Jonas was even more of a lone wolf than Ely had ever been.

Even with his own brothers, Jonas had always held himself separate to some degree. When they were kids, Jonas was the one who spent more time doing his own thing rather than playing in a group, who spent more time in his room, reading or studying, than out partying in college.

He'd become even more isolated after he left the police department, or so Garrett and Chance reported. Ely had been off to basic training back then, and had only heard of what happened to his brother.

Jonas didn't talk about what went down when he'd been caught in an undercover mess, but Ely knew it wasn't the way the papers had painted it. After being in a war, he knew exactly how the media could spin things.

Chloe shifted uncomfortably, taking another sip of her wine before she replied, and then he felt her reporter persona slip back in place, the distance reasserting itself.

He was willing to bet she knew something about James Rose that she didn't want to share.

"What are you thinking about?" he asked.

"There's a huge story breaking in a few hours," she said. "Rose's office is one of the ones that will be implicated."

"For what?"

"There's an embezzlement ring on the Hill. Several aides have been using their resources to siphon off funds from campaign coffers, using it for all manner of criminal business. I was clued in, and it's going to be a huge scandal," she said, her eyes lighting up.

"And Rose is in the middle of this?"

"Not him directly—but his aide, yes. You can't say anything about this, Ely, not until the story breaks. The arrests won't happen until morning, right before."

Ely smiled at how her color rose and her eyes brightened at the prospect of a hot story. She was passionate about her work. It was one of the things he loved about her.

"I won't say a word, I promise."

Still, his mind went to his brother and Tessa. They weren't together, but he hoped none of this would hurt the reputation of their agency.

"I can't say I'm surprised, and not even a little glad," he said. "That guy, the aide, Howie Stanton, is a slug. He came to the hospital the night Jonas was admitted and told him if he went near Tessa again, there would be bad consequences for the business."

"You're kidding. Well, the only bad consequences I see are ones coming down on him."

"I'll drink to that," Ely said, smiling.

Chloe was the kind of woman men dreamed about. Beautiful, smart and sexy, she knew how to do her job. It was one of the things he found sexiest about her.

Setting down her wine and reaching to take his glass, her eyes told him she didn't want to talk anymore. Loosening the tie of his robe, she trailed kisses down his chest, obviously intent on ending the conversation and returning the pleasure he'd provided her earlier.

Ely was determined to be a better man this time, to

not be as selfish and self-involved as he was when he'd first been with Chloe.

He also loved how she took control and pushed him back to the cushions, focused on her task.

She stroked his erection, looking at him with sheer pleasure and mischievous intent as her tongue darted out, tasting him, making him catch his breath.

"You stay put, Marine, and don't come until I tell you to. That's an order," she commanded with mock seriousness as she closed her mouth around him, sending his heart rate through the roof.

Ely gladly submitted. He was trained to take orders, and knew he wouldn't disobey this one if his life depended on it.

8

TESSA WAS EXHAUSTED and had actually nodded off for a few minutes curled up on the seat, her head cradled on Jonas's shoulder as Collins took them back to the store. The intimacy of the night and the dark in the restaurant was giving way to morning, allowing her some light to study him.

He was dozing, too, the manly lines of his face softened in sleep. She stared at the fullness of his mouth, which she couldn't get enough of. He looked peaceful, which was rare for him, she thought. They'd turned a corner of sorts, leaving the restaurant with the connection between them stronger.

Still, she worried. She hadn't asked Jonas the question she was dying to: why he had thought so badly about her after the accident. What had Howie said to him? Was her father up to his old tricks, controlling her life, and her love life?

Jonas was clearly under the impression that she had used him to get back at her father, or that her father had not thought he was "suitable" enough for her. There were things going on beneath the surface, and Tessa planned to find out what they were.

One thing she knew for sure was that Howie was a snake. She'd never liked him. Her father had suggested once that Howie had an interest in her, and that they would make a "solid match." The thought made her gag. Her father occasionally pushed one of his plastic political harpies in her direction, even though she never showed any interest.

Jonas said she didn't care about the cost to others. What costs? Could her father have threatened his business? She wouldn't put it past him.

Jonas didn't deserve any negative flak for what happened that night they'd been attacked. He stepped up to protect others, but leaned on no one. There was a loneliness at his core that made her ache to change it, to make him see how much she cared for him.

How much she loved him.

She wasn't afraid of the word. She'd often wondered if she would find anyone that she'd truly fall in love with. Then Jonas had walked into her shop, and she knew she had found the other half of her perfect combination.

She leaned in, snuggling into his shoulder again and loving how his arm came back around her so naturally. Turning her face into his chest, she inhaled, enjoying his natural scent, how it mingled with hers. Their bodies loved each other, but how could she convince him it was more than that?

Tessa had been fighting for what she wanted in life since she could remember, against her father, mainly. But also against the world in general or at least it always felt that way. Everyone always assumed the worst of her, and so she had once decided to walk the talk.

Even friends had often thought that as the daughter of a wealthy politician, she would never have to work for anything in her life. That it all would be handed to her.

It could have gone that way, had she made other decisions. She'd taken a very different path, and was glad for it. She hoped Jonas was coming to see who she really was, too.

"I can see you thinking," Jonas said sleepily, and she looked up to find he was watching her. "What about?"

"Just about you. Us."

"How so?"

"When I said, back at the restaurant, that we fit…I don't know. It just seemed like you were holding back. I was wondering why. And what you aren't telling me."

"We do fit. In some ways. And in others—we don't."

"Like?"

"Like physically. Otherwise, we come from very different worlds. You wouldn't be happy in mine, not for long. And vice versa."

"You hardly know me, Jonas. How do you know what would make me happy?"

"I've been through this before. My job is dangerous."

"I know that."

"And it's not great for relationships, let me tell you. If you and I were together, I might have to go on a job where I would be protecting someone, another woman, and living at her side for weeks—how would you deal with that? If the tables were turned, I wouldn't like it one bit."

"I agree, that would be hard. But there are four of

you, and you can divide the jobs accordingly, right? But if you *had* to do that, well, I guess I would just have to trust you. That's what we're talking about, right? It's not about different worlds, or your job or mine—it's about the fact that down deep, for whatever reason, you don't trust me. I'd like to know why. Do you really think I am so superficial that I would use you or anyone just to get at my father?"

Silence loomed between them, and the hurt spread from her heart to encompass her entirely, the same way the dark restaurant had done.

"I guess that's my answer," she said, twisting away.

"Tess, stop. Listen. I want to trust you, but I don't understand why you did what you did."

"Which was?"

He took a deep breath, and let it out. "Why you told your father's aide about our…kiss that night. Why you made it sound like I had initiated it, but more than that, I wonder why you told them at all? That was private, between us. I could only assume that—"

"That I had seduced you, and then run to tell my father about it as fast as I could and blamed it on you as a way to get out of having a bodyguard, and to shove it back in my father's face."

"Well, yeah."

"Here's a news flash, Jonas," she said. "I'm all grown up now, and I don't play those games anymore. I'm not my father. What you see is what you get."

"Well, your father was pretty pissed. He took me off the job, and his aide suggested that there could be trouble for me and my brothers if I got anywhere near you."

Tessa's mind went still. So she was right in her intuition. Her father had found a way to come between her and a man she wanted. Or had she done that all on her own? She hadn't been entirely forthright with Jonas from the start—he may have made the first move that night, but only because she had been pushing him to.

"Listen, I remember showing them where we were standing when the attack happened. Howie was there. Where you had fallen back, and how I had grabbed the bat, but I didn't say anything about us kissing. I guess they could have assumed, but I swear, I didn't tell them what was going on," she said. "And if anyone is playing games here, it's the senator. I told you what he did before, with my college boyfriend. He may like you working for him, but—"

"He wouldn't think I was good enough for his daughter," Jonas finished flatly, and she nodded.

"It's possible. He sees everything as reflecting on him, his career. But I don't think that. I never thought that. I never would use you. Not like you thought I did."

She wrapped her arms around herself, suddenly feeling cold. Then Jonas was there, pulling her in, holding her tight.

"I'm sorry, too. I was such a mess at the time, but I should have told you about my sight. I should have asked you before I assumed what had happened. I believe you, Tessa," he said, kissing her cheek gently and taking her arms from around her middle, twining them around his back.

She held on tight, seeking a deeper kiss, as if trying to let him know with her whole body how much she cared, and how much she never would cause him any pain, not if she could help it.

Heat rose between them, but this wasn't the place to pursue their newfound intimacy.

"I want to talk to my father as soon as possible about what happened that night, and set it right. I absolutely will not let him blame you for something that was not your fault at all," she said vehemently.

"Well, I wasn't exactly blameless, Tessa. And I would rather you didn't talk to your father, if that's okay. I can handle it. Let's set it aside for now, okay?"

"Okay," she said reluctantly. She wasn't surprised that he would want to handle it on his own, but still felt that she should do something to make it right.

The car stopped, and she frowned, hearing the sound of music playing out in the neighborhood, resisting the urge to argue with him for the moment.

"The electricity is back on," she said, but saw no evidence of that except for the music. The streetlights were still out, though the dawn was bathing the street in soft, after-storm light.

"Thank you so much, Collins. It was so nice to meet you. Tell Kate I will be in later today to check on her and help her get home," Tessa said, offering the older man a hug, which surprised him, and which he seemed happy to accept.

Jonas shook Collins's hand, and they waited as the car left.

"Well, at least the rain has stopped," he observed. "Where is the music coming from?"

"Looks like Lydia's having a party," she said, noting the candles and flashlights visible through the window of the tattoo parlor, and the sign in the window that announced a Blackout Party.

"Hey, where have you been?" a voice behind them asked, and Tessa turned to find her friend and neighbor Scott, who owned the deli across the street, walking toward them carrying a huge cooler.

"My friend Kate had a medical emergency," Tessa explained as Scott put the cooler down on the sidewalk. She gave him a hug and watched as he shook hands with Jonas. "It's been quite the adventure getting to her."

"How did you end up in scrubs?"

"We were soaked, so a nurse took pity on us."

"Nice. So your friend is okay?"

"Yes, we made it just in time, and she's fine. What's happening here?"

"They aren't predicting the power'll be back on until sometime tomorrow, so I had to use these cold cuts and salads before they went bad. Lydia had the idea to throw a blackout party for people around the neighborhood."

"Clever," Tessa said.

"Good to see you, too, Jonas. Wondered where you had gotten to, and was sorry to hear about your eyesight. Rotten break, but it's supposed to come back, right?" Scott asked, and Tessa saw Jonas straighten uncomfortably, nodding.

"Yes, that's what they're saying," Jonas confirmed briefly.

Tessa frowned. She should have told her friend Lydia to keep their previous conversation about Jonas private, but it was too late now.

"Come on in and have a sandwich or something. It's turned into a pretty good time," Scott said, picking up his cooler again.

"We just came from dinner, so—" Tessa started, but then Lydia appeared in her doorway, clapping excitedly.

"You're back, and you're okay! I'm so relieved. I went over to get you for the party, and the place was all closed up. I wondered where you'd got to," she said, and then smiling, noticed Jonas. "But now I can see you had other things to do."

Tessa rolled her eyes at her friend's unrestrained glee at seeing her with Jonas.

"We're really beat, Lydia," Tessa tried to beg off, but Lydia wasn't hearing any of it, and linked her arm through Jonas's, standing up on tiptoe to kiss his cheek.

She looked at Tessa and made a silent mime that Tessa could not quite decipher. She probably wanted all the details about her night with Jonas, knowing Lydia. Tessa nodded, letting her friend know she would catch up with her later.

Even Jonas's surly demeanor cracked at Lydia's happy welcome, and he offered her a kiss back.

Tessa knew he'd always enjoyed Lydia's visits, the two of them quipping and harassing each other like siblings.

Lydia didn't have any family, and Jonas didn't have any sisters. Tessa figured her friend enjoyed the brotherly back-and-forth she had developed with Jonas, and it gave Tessa yet another perspective on him, playing the big brother. She wondered what he was like with his own brothers, and hoped she'd have a chance to see them all together someday soon. If Jonas was interested in seeing her.

"Come on, it'll be fun." Scott led the way. "You can take some food for later."

Tessa laughed at her friend's insistence on pushing off his extra food and followed. Inside, she was greeted by several other business owners in the neighborhood as well as a few of the residential neighbors as music blasted from a speaker in the corner where someone had set up an iPod and food was set out everywhere.

Never one to miss a business opportunity, Lydia was also offering Blackout Special henna tats until the lights came back on.

"I have an opening. How about you let me paint you?" Lydia said to Tessa, catching Tessa staring at the sale sign on one of the food tables.

"No, thank you," she said.

"Jonas, don't you think Tessa should get a tat? I could do something very personal, and very tasteful... something only special people could see," Lydia said mischievously, and Tessa felt her cheeks heat.

"Lydia—" she warned.

"I think it could be fun," he said, surprising both women. "You game?" he asked Tessa.

"It's only henna," Lydia cajoled.

Tessa took good care of her skin. It was an important part of her business to show how well her products worked, but also to care for her health. She didn't sit in the sun for long periods of time and with no disrespect to her friend, had no interest in permanent ink. Still, she was feeling daring, and a temporary henna tat would be fun.

"Okay, why not?" she said. "I'll pick out yours, and you can tell Lydia what you want for me. We don't get to see until it's done."

Jonas looked slightly apprehensive. "No fair. I'm blind. I could end up walking around with who knows what on my forehead."

Tessa leaned in, feeling mischievous and whispered in his ear, "It wasn't your forehead I was thinking about," she teased, and then added, "I guess you'll have to trust me."

"Okay. I can do that," he said, and she knew they were talking to each other about far more than a tattoo.

"Actually, I think I have the perfect idea for both of you," Lydia said, and led them to the corner where she proceeded to sit them both down before her in comfortable chairs, and then grabbed a scarf from the shelf.

"Hey, what are you doing?" Tessa objected at first, as Lydia started to tie it around her eyes.

"It's supposed to be a surprise, right?"

"Lydia…"

"Trust me, Tessa."

Tessa sighed. It seemed to be the theme of her life at the moment, and she did trust Lydia, who winked at her as she tied the scarf around her face.

"This won't take long. It's a simple scroll, but it will work very well."

They listened to the music and conversations behind them then as Lydia worked, and Tessa laughed a few times, her palm tickling as Lydia painted there, and then turned her hand over, continuing.

"Um. I thought this would be small."

"It comes off in four to six weeks, Tessa. But you're going to like it, I promise."

Then she left Tessa to work on Jonas who was so quiet she thought maybe he had fallen asleep.

"There. Done!" Lydia pronounced, and Tessa wasn't sure she wanted to open her eyes, but when she did, she caught her breath in pleasure at the delicate scarlet-and-black scrolling that weaved its way around her hand and fingers, to the center of her palm, where it ended in a starburst.

She looked over to see Jonas grimacing. "Tell me she didn't paint flowers or kittens on my arms, please," he said.

Lydia snickered.

Tessa took his arm, and knew immediately what

Lydia had done, and she glanced up, meeting her friend's eyes.

Lydia shrugged. "It seemed right. You two fit," she said, echoing what Tessa had told Jonas earlier.

His was similar, but heavier, more manly, and also worked around his fingers, wrist and palm.

"You, uh, need to hold hands to really see how it comes together. It's a concept I developed while I was designing. You are the first ones I've tried it on. I call this one Completion."

Jonas shrugged and held out his hand, obviously disappointed that he couldn't see his. Tessa took it, and caught her breath. As their fingers wove together, their palms merging, so did the design. The scrolls connected into an intricate weave that created an entirely new design.

"Lydia, that's amazing…" Tessa breathed, and tried to explain it to Jonas, though she felt as if she couldn't do it justice. She wished so much he could see it, and said as much.

"Well, like I said, they last several weeks. And you said you had some signs your vision was coming back?" she asked Jonas.

"Yes."

"And you figure you'll be around in a few weeks?" Lydia asked baldly, to Tessa's horror.

He smiled. "Yeah, I hope so."

That made Tessa's heart stop.

"So there you go then." Lydia cleared her throat as they stood there, holding hands. "Okay, I'm going to go check on the party, and you guys can show off your tats, if you would, so it could drum up some business for me. You know, before you head upstairs to—"

"Lydia!" Tessa cut her friend off, laughing, and Lydia laughed, as well.

Gone, Tessa didn't let go of Jonas's hand as she went into his arms.

"I think you'll like it. It's very badass. Promise."

"Yeah, sounds like it," he said doubtfully, but found her lips and didn't seem overly concerned about the tattoo.

"I probably have soap that would remove it sooner than normal, if you like."

He squeezed her hand, and kissed her lightly. "I'm good with it. You want to mingle for a few minutes and then go upstairs?"

"Yeah. I'd like that."

Tessa wasn't sure she'd ever been this happy. Jonas seemed to have accepted that she wasn't his enemy, and more than that, he'd said he planned to be around. His sight was coming back, and he wanted to be with her.

Her father had tried to separate them, but fate had a different idea. Tessa was supposed to be with Jonas, she thought, looking down at how the designs on their hands merged into a perfect image that they showed off to guests who were suitably impressed.

They were together now, and she wouldn't let anything hurt them, least of all her father, she thought as they finally left the party and went back to her apartment, where she could have Jonas all to herself.

9

Norfolk, 6:00 a.m.

ELY STRETCHED ON the bed, twisted in sheets and slowly waking up to note he was alone in the bed. Then the sound of the shower filtered through his consciousness. He smiled, feeling satisfied and well used in the way only a night of great sex could offer.

Though it was more than sex this time, he acknowledged. He may not have been ready for more back when he first knew Chloe, but he was now.

He wanted something meaningful, something right, and he was amazed that it had been there all the while. He'd always imagined that he'd like to have a marriage, a home, just as his parents had. He'd just never found the woman he could imagine it with.

Or he had, and he'd almost lost her.

Swinging his legs over the side of the bed, he thought about joining Chloe in the shower.

Maybe in a minute.

Checking the clock, he realized he should probably touch base with his brothers. They'd been expecting him home the night before, but he could catch a flight back this morning, and be there by noon. After he talked with Chloe.

Finding his jeans pockets empty, he frowned, then smiled at the memory of the night before. His cell must have fallen in her car when they'd been fooling around.

Her landline was on the desk, and before calling his brothers, Ely decided to make reservations at a nice place down the road that served brunch. That way they could talk and make some plans. For the future.

He whistled as he opened drawers searching for a phone directory, only to find a diamond winking up at him. There was a flat card with writing under it—he looked, his hands cold. Picking it up, he read the delicate scroll, and then let it fall from his hands.

It was a wedding invitation.

Chloe was getting married. In four weeks.

He slammed the drawer shut, cursing under his breath. Clenching his fists in anger, he fought to gain control as the shower shut off.

He was a fool.

Opening the drawer again, he took out the ring to examine it more closely. Definitely an engagement ring. He set it on the dresser, carefully. Some poor slob had spent several months' pay on that rock.

Chloe came out from the shower, a towel wrapped loosely around her luscious form, her cheeks rosy. She was gorgeous as sin, but she wasn't the woman he thought she was. Not by a long shot.

"Beautiful ring your fiancé bought you—is that what you were stashing last night when we came back here?"

The color drained from her face, and her eyes

darkened so quickly he thought she might pass out, but then he recognized it was anger. At being caught.

"You went through my things?" she accused, her hands gripping the towel more tightly around herself.

"Not intentionally. I was going to make breakfast reservations, and had to use your phone since I dropped mine in the car last night while we were...well, you know what we were doing," he confessed. "Somehow I don't think it's my ethics that are in question here."

"You don't understand," she said, approaching him. "It was always you, but you didn't want anything permanent, you walked away. And I met him, Lance...and he reminded me of you. He's also a Marine. A good man."

"Then he deserves better than this," Ely said angrily. "How could you do this? So you used him because you couldn't have me, but then you screw around with me behind his back?"

"You're right, I know, I just...I planned to break it off with him, Ely. From the minute I saw you last night. That's why I took the ring off. So we can be together. I know I should have told you, but—"

"If you had told me, I never would have laid a hand on you," he said, feeling dirty, ashamed that he had been a part of this.

"I know. I'm sorry. But can't we just go from here? What we have together is so good. We're right together," she said, looking up into his eyes. She put a hand on his chest, and he stepped back, breaking the contact.

Ely stared at her as if he'd never really seen her before, and admitted that he didn't know her. Not really. He had only imposed his own perfect image of the woman he wanted, not the real woman she was.

"No, Chloe, nothing about this is right. It was a

fantasy I had, but that's over now. Whatever you do, have a nice life." He strode to the door, shaking his head at himself that he had even considered a future with her or with anyone.

"Ely, no—" she called after him desperately, but he was dressed and already gone.

BACK IN HER APARTMENT, Tessa was joyfully preparing to experience a fantasy she'd been harboring about Jonas for weeks. She turned on the hot water and sprinkled something in the tub that immediately infused the air around them with a sultry, spicy scent.

"What is that?" he asked, kissing and nuzzling as he pulled her scrubs off as she undressed him, too.

"Gardenia musk bath oil. It's part of my new erotic collection."

"I can't say I'm one for scented baths, but I don't think I care so long as it's you and me in there," he said with a chuckle, letting his hands drift over every curve of her body.

"Here, let me help you in. Be careful," she said, stepping into the deep bath and helping him get in safely, as well.

Her tub was huge. He'd always teased her about it, why one small woman needed such a large tub, but it made sense for someone in her line of business, he supposed.

He had also secretly fantasized about sharing it with her.

He sank back into the hot water with a groan.

"Feels good?"

"Everything with you feels good."

They relaxed into the heat, and she wanted to keep hearing him talk, liking the sound of his voice.

"Tell me about your brothers," she said as she washed his shoulders.

"You met Garrett?"

"Definitely," she said, unable to repress a sigh.

Jonas laughed. "I take it he was a brick wall?"

"That's putting it mildly. I don't think he approves of me," she said, the dark and the tenor of the conversation drawing out a need to confess. "I feel awful that I distracted you, Jonas. I know you might not have lost your sight if it weren't for me."

"He doesn't think that. Hell, *I* don't think that. I was the one who lost focus. I can't blame you for that," he said.

"I still feel responsible, at least in part. I didn't take my father's concerns seriously enough. We put up with that kind of thing all the time growing up, and it never came to anything. I guess I never really thought anything would actually happen."

"That's why I was there. You weren't supposed to worry about it. I let you down, Tessa. You and your father," he said insistently.

She didn't comment. She never felt as if he'd let her down until that morning, when he told her he thought she'd used him.

"Gare does like you, actually," Jonas said, though she wasn't sure if he was just being polite. "But, in order, from youngest to oldest, it's Chance, Ely, me and then Garrett. Chance is the only one who inherited my mom's light coloring. The rest of us are dark, like Dad. Chance is the risk-taker. When we were kids, we thought we were picking on him by hiding his favorite stuff in the tree out in our backyard and making him climb up to get it, but he loved it. He was never afraid of anything," Jonas said with clear affection in his voice.

"And Ely?"

"He's the ex-Marine—though every time I say that, he'll say, 'There are no ex-Marines,'" Jonas mimicked. "Ely is the quiet one, the strategist. Garrett is the prototypical big brother. He thinks it's his job to watch over us all."

"And which are you? How do you place yourself in that lineup?"

"I've never really thought about it."

"Can I take a stab at it?"

"Sure."

"I think you're the loner. You may not be the oldest, but you're the one who takes the heaviest load on yourself, and you don't like to bother anyone to help you carry it."

"That's a romantic notion," he said, sounding uncomfortable.

"Not at all. I didn't say it was a good thing. Everyone needs help sometimes, dealing with life's burdens. But you think you can carry them alone," she said bluntly.

"Garrett was saying something similar. Maybe it's true, but it's who I am."

"Losing your sight must have been even more challenging in that respect, making you depend on others for a change. Like having to call me when you hurt your foot."

He was quiet for a few beats, and she wondered what he was thinking.

What Jonas was thinking was how he was in way too deep, and how he had really messed this up. He was falling for Tessa—hard—and his being here was a lie, at least to an extent.

He was a coward. He hadn't told her about her father's

call because he knew it would be the end for them. But he had to make things right.

He'd take this time with her, right now, and then he'd go, he knew, feeling her hands slip over him. He wasn't strong enough to leave now, but soon. And he'd make it right, he vowed to himself, one way or another.

"Sit up a bit," she said, and they maneuvered so that she was on her knees behind him.

"What are you doing?"

"I have some massage oil you're going to love," she told him, and the same scent that was in the bath was suddenly twice as pungent as her hands made their way expertly over his back and shoulders, massaging and working each muscle individually.

"Wow, you're good at that," he sighed, his heart aching while his body sang. "I don't care what scent it is, just don't stop."

"I love touching you," she said close to his ear.

He felt her breasts press into his back as her arms reached around and held him in a curiously tender gesture.

"I love you touching me," he said roughly.

A second later she was sitting in between his thighs, and she took his hand, putting some oil into his palm.

"Do me," she said sexily, and he groaned.

"With pleasure."

He did as she did, smoothing the oil everywhere, seeking out any tension, knots or spots that he could massage to tenderness, slipping around the front to do the same to her breasts. He ran his hands over her to memorize every inch of her, hoping that when all was said and done, this wouldn't be the last time he touched her.

"I don't think I can ever take a bath alone again," she said, leaning back against him.

"Time to get out?" he asked, kissing her neck.

"Absolutely," she purred in a vixen voice that turned him on even more.

She handed him a towel and helped him out. Somehow, having Tessa assist him didn't bother him as much now. He didn't feel needy or dependent, but connected. And any excuse to touch her was okay with him. They dried each other, touching and driving each other crazy in the process.

"Bedroom," Jonas growled as she licked a straight path down his chest in a straight line to his erection.

"Come with me."

They walked in hand in hand, and Jonas found his way to the bed, sliding up to sit on the pillows, wondering why she didn't join him.

"What are you doing?"

Then she was there, straddling him and rubbing her finger along his lips.

"Taste."

He did, licking his lip and then sucking her finger into his mouth.

"Mmm. Sweet."

"It's my signature honey dust…you like?"

"I like how you taste with or without it, but it's very nice, yes," he said, tired of talking.

He pulled her closer, his mouth tracing a trail of the dust from the pulse at her throat to the tip of her breast, where he tasted deeply, drawing on her nipple until she was whimpering.

"Oh, you are tasty," he murmured.

"It's for both of us," she said, her voice trembling

as she lifted, and the next thing Jonas felt was a light, tickling sensation that made his cock surge.

"What—"

"More honey dust—applied with the feather that comes with every jar. So I can taste you," she said.

His mind blanked as her tongue was the next thing he felt, licking and darting out to taste until he was strained to the limit and fighting for control.

"Please, Tessa," he said, unsure how much more he could take.

"Oh, I do like that," she said in a sultry tone, dragging her nails up and down his thighs. "So sexy, Jonas."

She took him whole then, making his entire body arch off the bed.

"That's enough, you vixen," he said, and she laughed as he pulled her up and over him.

He loved her laugh.

"I never imagined this side of you," he said, enjoying how she took control. "I like it."

"There's so much more, Jonas. I like to play," she said as she rolled the condom over his erection with warm, loving hands before settling herself over him.

"I need you," she said, meaning every word as she took him inside with a sigh.

Jonas couldn't speak, the perfection of it robbing him of words. If only he could see her, it would be perfect, but he could imagine her blond curls riotous, her cheeks flushed, lips red from sucking him. Her hands planted on his chest as she moved, and he could picture her breasts moving as she did.

"So good," she whispered, rocking gently until she started to make the soft crying sounds he loved.

He covered her breasts with his hands and then dived in to lick away the rest of the sweet dust, sucking at her tender skin until she rocked faster, her cries becoming louder. His breath came in short panting bursts, his body feeling like a bow strung too tight.

"Yeah, sweetheart," he crooned and pushed his hips up as she rocked over him. She planted her hands on his shoulders, finding the rhythm she needed, and he held her hips, jackhammering up to meet her as they both lost any sense of control, pushed over the edge of a hard, simultaneous orgasm that left them shaking and panting as she fell against his chest, their bodies still deeply joined.

"More," was all he said, easing her over to her stomach and lifting her hips, positioning her on all fours before him. He felt primal, possessive, taking her this way.

"Tessa, you are every man's fantasy come to life," he said, running his hands over her completely, teasing every inch of her.

"I only want to be yours."

Regret and need for her warred inside him, and he pressed his face against her back where he trailed kisses down her spine, making her shiver as his fingers did delightful things between her legs. She was slick from her first orgasm and his touch, and yet she needed more, too.

"Please, Jonas," she begged shamelessly, sighing in sheer happiness as he slid inside, burying himself deep in response to her request.

"You're perfect, Tessa," he said reverently, still touching her back, her thighs, until his hands rested on her hips as he thrust faster.

Jonas massaged her perfect ass as he moved inside her, then reached down to circle his fingers around the slick, hot nub in a way that would drive her crazy.

"Jonas, oh…yes," she managed to breathe, easing back against him for more, which he was happy to provide. His balls pulled tight, feeling full and heavy, his body hot.

"Come for me, Tess, again," he said raggedly, increasing the tempo until every muscle inside fisted around him, clenching and releasing as they both shouted out their mutual release.

They rode it out, not wanting to stop until they fell back to the bed.

Tessa burrowed into his chest as his arms came around her, hugging her in close. They nestled and nuzzled, lost in a cocoon of intimacy that closed out the rest of the world.

JONAS KNEW WHAT HE had to do, but it was the hardest thing he'd ever contemplated. Previously, he thought leaving the police force had been the hardest decision of his life, but it didn't even come close to leaving Tessa.

He wanted to do nothing more than go back to her, to lie in her arms and wake up with her, but he couldn't. Not until this mess was straightened out.

Jonas liked James, or thought he did. Listening to Tessa's stories about how he'd wrecked her relationships and tried to keep her from starting her business—what kind of parent did that?

Jonas's father and mother had encouraged all the boys to be who they were, regardless. Hard work, discipline, loyalty—these were the things that counted. How they dressed, who their friends were, what they wanted to do with their lives—Jonas's parents never put any obstacles in their way. They still lived in the family home in Fishtown, and Jonas saw them regularly, not only for holidays.

But more importantly, Jonas had to step away before he did further damage. He couldn't be Rose's weapon of choice anymore, and certainly not when it came to Tessa.

She probably wouldn't want anything to do with him when she found out, but that was how it was. He'd brought it on himself. All he could do was tell her the truth and let the chips fall where they may.

Feeling around on her kitchen counter, he knew she kept notepaper by the phone, and found that and a pen.

Swallowing hard, he wrote:

Tessa: I didn't mean to lie to you. Not really. It was part of the job. I never expected to fall for you—that wasn't part of the job, either. I know it was wrong for us to be together when I am still working for your father, but I want you to know, what happened between us last night was real. I hope you can forgive me someday,
Love,
Jonas

He scrawled out the message and left the paper on the table, and picked up the phone to call his brother.

As he dialed, Jonas gasped, the pain in his head nearly doubling him over. The room spun, and he gripped the edge of the counter, and to his amazement, he saw it—saw it all. The marble pattern of the counter, the ray of sunlight cutting across his hands, the note with his crooked scrawl on it.

Then darkness again as his stomach lurched, nausea and disorientation turning his hands cold.

His vision was returning? Like this? His hands shook

10

TESSA WOKE UP alone, and lay still in bed, smiling. The night before had been like some kind of wild fantasy, traversing the city by all means available, and ending up here, with the man of her dreams in her arms.

Her body ached in a delicious way from their love-making, and she stretched, yawning and wishing he was here with her so she could curl around him and go back to sleep. Yeah, right. Sleep wasn't exactly what she wanted right at the moment.

Where was Jonas? Peeking at the clock, she saw it had only been about an hour, and she wondered what he was up to. She didn't hear the shower or anyone moving around. In fact, it was too quiet.

Concerned, she got up and grabbed a robe from her dresser, padding into the other room. Nothing there.

Then she heard a groan and walked quickly to the kitchen where she gasped in fright, finding Jonas sitting on the floor, holding his head.

"Oh, my God, Jonas," she said, rushing to his side as he slumped down to the floor, his face white.

"Call my brother," he said weakly, not sounding at all like himself. She could see he was in terrible pain.

Tessa called emergency first, and then his office, hoping to hell someone was there.

"Berringer Security," a man's voice answered.

"This is Tessa Rose—is this Garrett?"

"It is," Garrett said, sounding wary.

"I'm calling for your brother Jonas—"

"Is he okay? I just got into the office, and the place looks like a wrecking ball hit it. The first-aid kid is out, and I've been calling the hospitals, since he isn't answering his phone—"

"He's with me," she said, interrupting. "He's been with me all night, but I don't know if he's okay. I've called the paramedics. I found him here on my kitchen floor, and he's holding his head, and somewhat incoherent."

"Are they there yet?"

"I hear the sirens now."

"I'll meet you at St. Mark's Medical, and I'll call his doctor. You take care of him, Tessa."

"I will."

She didn't see the slip of paper on the counter until she hung up the phone, and scanned it quickly.

Her heart broke, and she forced away tears. Jonas had been leaving her? With a note?

And he had been lying to her?

Now was not the time for this. Pushing the pain and the anger aside, she kneeled by Jonas and took his hand. His skin was cold, clammy, and worry clashed with the other emotions that rocked her.

"It'll be okay, they're coming, and Garrett is meeting

us at the hospital," she reassured, even as she looked up at the counter again, seeing the note, as if to confirm she'd actually seen it, and not just imagined it.

He'd been working for her father? How? Why?

Dozens of questions erupted, none of which could have answers while she sat here with him.

Paramedics knocked hard at the downstairs door, and she raced to meet them. Just a few minutes later, they were taking Jonas to the hospital, and she was left standing in the kitchen in her robe, staring at the note.

Daylight glared through the window, but she barely noticed, numb to her core.

No doubt her exhaustion had something to do with magnifying her feelings, but her disappointment and hurt that Jonas had deceived her was cutting deep.

Right now she couldn't indulge that pain. She needed to go to the hospital and at least make sure he was okay. Then she'd come back here and nurse her own wounds.

It was a particular form of self-torture, but she reached for the note, staring at it.

She felt stupid, used and vulnerable. Was that how he had felt when he thought she had done the same to him? Was it really a job, or was this just revenge?

Putting aside the pity party, she padded into the shower, heart heavy, needing to wash his scent from her body, but at the same time, it was so incredibly painful to do so. She wanted him to come back. To hold her.

Jonas didn't want her. He was only doing a job.

She'd been so sure that they had something perfect, something incredible.

It was only sex, she thought morosely, pausing before she turned on the water, giving in to tears. The last eighteen hours or so seemed like a dream. One that had left her with a rude awakening.

She soaked herself beneath the spray as tears flowed. She'd allow herself a few minutes to cry over what she'd thought was something wonderful, but promised herself that after she left the shower, she wouldn't waste one more tear on him.

She squeezed a fragrant honey-almond liquid soap on her loofah, and washed as if intent on scrubbing his touch from her skin. That brought on more tears. It would be some time before she could forget how he'd touched her, and how she'd responded.

But she would, eventually.

Getting out of the shower, she wanted only to go to bed, to lose herself in sleep where she wouldn't have to think about any of it, but, she had to get dressed and go to the hospital. In spite of it all, she had to know if he was all right. As she dropped the towel, her phone rang.

News about Jonas? She looked at the caller ID and saw her father's number on the screen.

Her anger flared anew, and she answered.

"Hello, Dad," she said tersely.

"Hello, sweetheart. I was calling to make sure you're okay."

"Just drop the act, Senator." She knew he hated it when she called him that.

"What's going on, Tessa?"

He had the gall to act exasperated, as if she was being unreasonable.

"Why would you be worried? You hired Jonas to babysit me until you got back, right?"

Her father sighed heavily. "He told you?"

"Yes, though not everything. Don't ever do that to me again," she said, her voice breaking.

"Honey, what's wrong? What did he do?"

"He didn't do anything," she sobbed.

Just broke her heart in two—the both of them together had done that, her father and Jonas.

"He's at the hospital, St. Mark's. I think something is happening with his vision, but it didn't seem right. I found him barely conscious on my kitchen floor," she said, unable to stop tears from springing forth, and hating it.

"I'm on my way back there now. I'll be arriving in an hour or so. You stay where you are."

He cut the call before she could say goodbye, and hung up. She was dazed and tired down to her bones, but she had to get to the hospital. Dressing quickly, she heard more knocking at her front door, rushed to answer.

She found Lydia, looking frantic.

"I saw paramedics taking someone out—what's going on?"

"It's Jonas. I don't know, something was wrong with his head. I just found him here," she said, and burst into tears again.

Lydia hugged her, and dug out a wad of tissues from her purse. "Oh, honey, it will be okay. Let me get my car, I'll drive, and you tell me what's going on, okay?"

Tessa nodded, relieved to have one person she could count on in her life. Lydia had never let her down. Maybe she should have listened more closely to her friend, who was a classic commitmentphobe. Lydia had several lovers, and didn't believe in getting too attached to any of them. Tessa attributed that to her rather rough upbringing, mostly in foster homes, but she also knew that Lydia was into some kinky stuff, sexually speaking.

Way more than Tessa ever experienced.

None of that mattered. How her friend ran her sex life wasn't Tessa's concern. Lydia had always been there for her, and that's what mattered. In fact, Lydia was like the sister Tessa had never had.

As they made their way to the hospital, she told Lydia all of it, and her friend shook her head in disbelief.

"I can't believe he would do that. Why? It's clear he's crazy about you—why not just tell you the truth?"

"He was obviously more worried about upsetting my father than he was about being honest with me," Tessa said dully as they got into an elevator at the hospital. "I guess it's good to know where his loyalties lie."

"I think you all need to sit down and talk once this is over, and we know he's okay. It sounds to me like there's a lot of confusion in the air, and you can't make any assumptions until it's all out."

"It's pretty clear, Lydia. He left me a note—he was leaving."

"And you said he told you he cared, and that what happened between you was real. Hold on to the good things, Tessa, not just the bad."

Tessa grumbled something and yawned as the doors opened in front of the nurses' station.

They got the information for Jonas's room, and he was permitted visitors.

"I don't know. Maybe this isn't a good idea," Tessa said, stopping halfway down the hall.

Lydia took her hand. "You have to see him to make sure he's okay, at least. Then we can go, okay?"

Tessa nodded, her stomach in knots. She was worried sick about him on top of everything else, and Lydia was right. She had to make sure he was okay before she could let herself be angry with him.

They walked down to the room, where a nurse came out, her cheeks flushed, eyes bright. She smiled at Tessa and Lydia.

"Is this Jonas Berringer's room?"

"Oh, yes," the young nurse said, giggling, her cheeks flushed.

Lydia rolled her eyes at Tessa, but they soon found out what had the young woman so flustered.

Walking into the private room where Jonas was sitting up in bed, looking none too happy in a hospital gown, Tessa saw why the young woman was so worked up.

"Oh, my," Lydia said, seeming flustered herself.

Four big men filled the room, standing around Jonas's bedside. There was so much testosterone that Tessa could have bottled it and made soap. All the male gazes turned to look at them.

One she recognized as Garrett, and from Jonas's descriptions, could guess which ones were Ely and Chance, though she didn't know the fourth.

"Tessa," Jonas said, and she realized after a second that he had turned to see her.

He could *see* her.

She lifted a hand to her mouth, her eyes flooding.

"Jonas, you can see me?" she said, awed.

He nodded. "Mostly. Everything is still kind of fuzzy around the edges, and shapes are blurring together, but yeah, I can see you," he confirmed. "Or a blob that more or less looks like you."

"You sure know how to talk up the ladies, Jonas," one of his brothers, the one she assumed was Chance, teased.

They looked at each other for several long minutes, until someone cleared his throat.

"Jonas, there's no need for you to stay. The initial pain and dizziness you experienced was normal, if uncomfortable," the man Tessa didn't know explained.

His doctor, obviously.

Jonas said, grimacing, "You're telling me."

"The meds I gave you should take care of that. You just had too much blood surging to that area of your brain as the vessels opened up," he explained.

Another of his brothers made some sideways comment about that being surprising, as they thought it would have all been elsewhere.

Jonas threw his brothers a dirty look, and then nodded to the doctor. "Thanks, Matt."

He met Tessa's eyes again, and Garrett spoke up. "Okay, I guess we can maybe go get a cup of coffee while Tessa and Jon talk," he said, almost pushing his younger brothers out of the room.

They all smiled at Tessa and Lydia on their way out, and Tessa noticed Lydia's gaze had not wandered far from Ely.

"Mind if I join you? I don't think I'm needed here, either," she said, introducing herself to the men as they all exited the room, leaving Tessa and Jonas together.

Tessa inched farther into the room.

"Close the door?"

"Okay," she agreed.

When she turned back to him, she didn't know what to say. It was all too much to process.

"I can't believe you're here. That you came," he said.

"I had to know that you were all right. You scared the life out of me," she admitted.

Among other things.

"I'm sorry, Tessa."

"For what? For thinking I used you? For lying to me? For not telling me you were working with my father? For leaving me with a *note?*" she accused, pacing back and forth by the bed, the emotions flooding back. "God, Jonas…it's no wonder you didn't think we have any chance together. You were undermining us at every turn."

"I know," he said, and seemed to struggle to say anything else.

Silence loomed between them.

"I thought your brothers were out of town," she said, needing to say something.

"Ely was already on his way back, and I guess Garrett called Chance as soon as he was off the phone with you, and he was also on his way back from New York. Not necessary, but—"

"They're your brothers."

She realized then that his choices didn't just have to do with his loyalty to her father, but his loyalty to his family, as well.

No doubt he was worried about how her father's displeasure would affect their agency, and she couldn't completely blame him for that, but at the same time, she wondered where she fit in. He seemed as if he was willing to hurt her before any of the rest.

Not a glowing start for a relationship.

"Can you come closer, Tessa? It's still hard for me to make out faces at a distance. Or even up close for that matter," he added dryly.

She walked to the side of the bed, and her heart stuttered at the sight of the tattoo on his hand. The other half of hers.

"Was it all a lie? A game? Last night, did you really even fall and hurt yourself? Or was that just a way to get me to come to you?" She felt like a fool as it was.

He shook his head. "Both. I knew it wasn't a good idea to take your father up on his request, but I also couldn't say no."

"Why?"

"Because I owed him for messing up the first time, and because it would allow me to see you again. Because I was worried about you being alone if something was wrong. I was trying to convince myself that you had been using me, and this was just an opportunity to set things right with your father. But it was all an excuse to be with you."

"You were worried about your agency."

"That, too. Your father's aide made it clear that there would be repercussions if I saw you again."

"Howie?"

"Yeah. So I kept my distance. And then, there you were in my apartment yesterday, and…I wanted you. I hadn't been able to stop thinking about you for a minute after the night of the attack."

"So why didn't you tell me that?"

"I didn't trust your motives," he admitted, shaking his head. "I had been through it once before. Fell in love with someone back when I was on the force, and it went bad. Really bad. I found out she was using me just to get information. It nearly got people killed. It was why I left the force."

"So you saw me as doing the same thing?"

"Sort of. I had screwed up once in my past, and people suffered for my mistake. I didn't want that to happen again. I tried to talk myself into believing it was your fault, but I think that was because in the end, I really was afraid you'd never really be interested in me for the long run. That it was just a fling."

"What, some kind of bodyguard-fantasy thing?"

"It happens," he said flatly, and she assumed he had some experience in that area, too.

Jealousy flared in her chest. She didn't like to think about women he guarded coming on to him, and remembered their earlier conversation about his work.

Maybe she wouldn't handle that all as coolly as she imagined.

"Well, I don't know what to do, Jonas. I…care about you. A lot. But it hurt so much to find that note."

"I was trying to do the right thing. I assumed once you knew, you'd want me gone. I couldn't blame you for that."

"You didn't even give me a chance. Just like he does, you just made my decisions for me," she said, throwing her arms up and walking away, then back to the bed.

It was painful being this close to him and not being able to touch, even though her heart was bruised and her mind wary.

"You're right. I didn't. I don't know, Tessa. I've never felt this way about anyone, and I don't know how to deal with it."

Tessa was torn. Everything he said now helped her understand, but she didn't know if she could trust him again—what about the next time he felt he had to keep information from her, or he lied to her to "protect" her?

She was tired of being manipulated and controlled by the men in her life, and how they always seemed to think it was for her own good.

"I don't know either, Jonas. I…I thought I loved you, but now I don't know if I really knew you. Maybe it was only sex," she said, and jumped when his hand reached out to grab hers.

Tessa caught her breath, looking down at how the scrolls Lydia had painted on them entangled, completed each other.

She was so confused.

"No, it wasn't just that. I know I don't deserve another chance, Tessa, but I'd like a chance to do this right. To show you that I…I think I love you, too."

Tears welled and dropped down onto their hands where they were clasped together on the bed, and she couldn't find anything else to say.

She wanted to believe him more than anything, but she didn't know who she could trust anymore. For the moment, she just stayed there, quiet, and held his hand. She was afraid that if she let go, there'd be no going back.

IN THE HOSPITAL'S WAITING lounge, Ely sat with his brothers, waiting for Jonas to emerge from his room. It was taking some time. He was willing to wait, relieved that his brother was going to be okay. Garrett and Chance were in the corner talking about the job Chance had just returned from, and Ely was just…waiting.

He didn't have all the details, but Ely only needed to look at his older brother's face when Tessa had come in. Jonas had fallen, and fallen hard.

He'd also screwed up royally, by the looks of it. Not that Ely had anything to brag about in that area.

"It gives the phrase 'get a room' a whole new meaning," Tessa's friend, Lydia, said, from her seat beside him as she glanced back at the door.

Ely had to chuckle. Lydia was…different. Not his

type, not by a long shot, but she was nice enough. And funny.

"Yeah, I guess Jonas had some explaining to do."

"I hope they work it out. They really are perfect together, even though I don't buy into the whole soulmates thing. I have a feeling Tessa is just what your brother needs in his life," Lydia said. "Some people can make it work."

Ely watched the length of the tattoo that seemed to move as she lifted her hand, bringing coffee to lips that sported one piercing at the edge. His gaze landed on the tiny moon at the corner of her mouth.

She slanted her eyes up. "Yes?"

He broke the stare. "Sorry. Just admiring your tattoos."

Or wondering at them, he thought. He had one tat on his shoulder blade. It was something he did as a right of passage in the Marines, but Lydia's practically covered every inch of her skin. He wondered if that was literally true, tracing the inked patterns that dipped beneath her clothing, and realized he was staring again.

"Sorry, again," he said, meeting her quizzical gaze.

She grinned, apparently not offended at all. "No problem. I get that a lot."

He imagined that was true.

Her black hair hung to her shoulders like a satin sheet, her skin pale, but covered in ink. Her eyes, though… they sparkled with humor. And mischief.

"Did you do all that ink yourself?"

"Some of it. What I could reach anyway," she said with a wink.

Ely wasn't quite sure what else to say as Lydia grabbed his arm and directed his attention to the news on the TV in the corner. When she popped up and ran to turn up the volume, he couldn't help but notice what a sleek little body she had, though the black lace and leather she wore didn't hide a whole lot.

When she backed away from the television, Ely stiffened, feeling as if he had just been punched in the gut.

Chloe's face filled the screen.

She looked, as always, perfect. Makeup hid any shadows that might have cropped up under her eyes from the night before, and when she peered into the camera, she might as well have been looking directly at him.

"You know her," Lydia said. A statement, not a question. She was observant, and Ely knew he was not easy to read. That came with his training.

"Not well," he answered, and it was the truth.

They all turned their attention to the broadcast of the arrests being made in the Senate and House, a total of fifteen aides taken into custody in an embezzlement scam that was rocking the Hill.

The aides were all highly placed, and were privy to some of the most secret information handled by their official's offices. There was speculation about the selling of secrets as well as misdirecting funds.

Ely was rapt, watching as Chloe delivered the news. She didn't miss a beat. She was also wearing her ring. Maybe Lance would fare better than he had. He hoped so.

"Wow, that's huge. I can believe that slimeball Stanton was involved, though. He's come by the store a few times and he always gave me the creeps," Lydia said, shuddering. "He wanted me to schedule him for a tat, and I refused. There was always something about him."

"People are not always what they seem," Ely said,

feeling as if he'd been shaken out of a trance as Chloe's image disappeared from the screen.

When he looked up, he raised an eyebrow as he recognized the formidable figure of Senator Rose walking by the waiting room, heading toward Jonas's door.

Ely met Garrett's gaze across the room; he noticed, as well.

"Think we should go give Jonas some backup?" Ely asked.

Garrett shook his head. "Let them figure it all out."

Lydia had pulled her knees up to her chin on the chair, and he was again distracted by the ink that flowed down her slim legs, peeking out from under the edge of the tights she wore, that stretched only midthigh.

Everything about her was firm and lithe, and she turned her eyes to his to catch him staring, again.

She smiled, looking a lot like a cat who would like to lick the dish clean.

"I could use another cup of coffee. You want to walk down with me?" she asked.

"Sure. I could use another cup myself. It's been a long couple of days," he elaborated unnecessarily, but there was something about the small Goth woman that threw him.

It was unusual. Maybe he was losing his touch in civilian life—he'd been completely taken in by Chloe, and now Lydia was making him feel unsteady, as well.

He watched as she unfolded herself from the seat, though at full height, and even in the clunky, black platform shoes she wore, the top of her head was barely level with his chin.

They paused outside the waiting room and watched

as the senator knocked on Jonas's door and then disappeared inside the room.

"The suspense is killing me," Lydia said, nibbling at a nail that was painted black. Delicate, inked vines trailed down her slim fingers.

"C'mon, let's go get that coffee," Ely said, putting his hand to her shoulder, and he registered a shock of surprise at his response to the softness of her inked skin, and how small she felt, as well as strong.

Her eyes met his, and there was heat there.

He pulled his hand back. After what he went through with Chloe the night before, he wasn't getting involved with anyone again for a long time, let alone someone who was clearly so...odd.

He was sure his response was just some kind of backlash from his disappointment the night before—and that wasn't fair to Lydia, either, who seemed like a perfectly nice person.

She was also Tessa's friend, and with any luck, Tessa would be part of their family one day soon.

Ely pasted on a polite smile and made a promise to himself to stop staring at the strangely attractive woman who stepped inside the elevator with him. Unlike his brother, he learned his lessons the first time.

11

"MAY I INTERRUPT?" a voice intruded from behind, and Tessa turned as they saw her father come inside.

"Dad," she said, and Jonas felt the sting of it as she wrenched her hand from his.

"Sir," he said as well, but more cautiously. Why was Rose here?

"They said you have some of your sight back, Jonas. That's good news," James said, walking up close to the bed and hugging his daughter. Tessa didn't hug him back.

Jonas couldn't make out faces well enough to see Tessa's reaction, but she didn't say anything.

"I'm fine, Senator. You didn't need to come."

James Rose sighed, sounding very tired. "Do you mind if I pull up a chair? It was a long flight, and unlike you young guns, this old man can't go twenty-four hours at a time."

He saw Tessa move then, pulling a chair up for her father, who sat.

"Truth is, I should have come the first time you were in the hospital, that night of the attack. Maybe that would have solved a lot of problems. This time, I needed to make sure I could help clarify what was going on for you two," he said, though Jonas didn't know what he was talking about.

"I think we're clear, Dad," Tessa said. "You threatened Jonas's business if he came near me again, accusing him of failing to protect me the first time. Then you used my attraction to him to have him watch me last night, too, but why? Why would you do such a thing to us?" she asked, her voice quavering.

"Ah, I'm so sorry, Tessie. I take it you haven't seen the news yet?"

They shook their heads, mystified. What did the news have to do with anything?

"It's a grand mess, and I only heard about it all yesterday morning," he started, and then filled them in on the embezzlement scam, and Howie's part in it. "It's why I had to cut my trip short and come back. This will take some sorting out."

"So you sent Jonas to stay with me? Why? It's not like I was involved," Tessa said, and Jonas couldn't figure out the connection, either.

"There's more than the news made known. I got some of my people on the job as soon as I was told, and they discovered something…disturbing. I have enough information to suggest that Howie orchestrated the attack on you the night Jonas lost his sight," the senator said with a sigh. "He paid off the guy who broke in. There's a money trail."

"But why?"

"It's my fault. It's *all* my fault, actually," James said, sounding tired and old in a way that surprised Jonas.

It must have surprised Tessa, too, as he saw her draw closer to her father.

"What do you mean?"

"You know I pushed Howie in your direction, Tessa. I thought he would be a good match, though it was obviously you didn't even like the man. He made it quite clear to me that he wanted to ask you out, however, and at the time, I thought he was a reliable, solid kind of guy. He'd been with my office for almost three years."

"So you think he attacked us because he was… jealous?"

"Well, I don't think he was in love with you, no offense, Tessie, but I think he wanted to get in as close to me as he could. He was like the lot of them, power hungry, and willing to do anything to get it. Steal, resort to criminal activity, even. I was fool enough not to see what was happening under my nose. I think he viewed Jonas as a threat to that—noticed the attraction you two had."

Jonas thought about what the aide had said to him at his bedside that night. Howie Stanton had obviously been the one manipulating the situation, not Tessa or her father.

Jonas was suddenly very angry at himself—if he had not jumped to conclusions and just believed what he was told, maybe he could have found that out sooner. But then he remembered James's phone call—it seemed to confirm his beliefs about what was going on.

His head started to ache slightly, and he took a deep breath.

"So how much of what he said to me that night was true?"

"Well, I wasn't happy to hear what happened, of course. Though Howie played me, too, and made it all sound much more salacious than it was—hopefully, anyway," he said, looking at Jonas.

Jonas couldn't see his expression clearly, but felt the weight of it. He was starting to speak, when Tessa interrupted.

"There was nothing salacious about what happened between me and Jonas," she said hotly. "And it was my fault, not Jonas's. I had been trying to get him to notice me. To respond to me. But he was so…businesslike. Then that night, things just…happened. But I didn't do it to lure him in, or to get back at you. I know you probably don't believe that, either of you, but it's true."

"You think I was angry at him because you two had…an attraction to each other? I don't care about that," her father claimed.

"Then why?" Jonas asked.

"I fired you because you didn't do your job, Jonas. You didn't protect her, and you could have been killed! Both of you," he added. "I wasn't thinking straight, and I knew if I went to the hospital, I'd say things I might regret. But I never told Howie to level any kind of threat, and I wasn't angry that you and Tessa were attracted to each other. I never forbade you to see her."

Jonas didn't detect anything but sincerity in the senator's voice.

"I let you down. I put her in danger, and you're right about that," admitted Jonas, understanding how the aide had manipulated things to his own ends. "I should have spoken to you directly, sir. I'm sorry about that, about assuming the worst about you, and about Tessa. I hope this hasn't damaged our friendship too severely."

"Well, the girl did have a history of liking to rub things in my face," the senator said. "But if you hurt her, I—"

Tessa huffed, inserting herself into the fray.

"Hello? I'm sitting right here? It's all very well and good how you two are making nice, but what about me? I don't care if you think you are protecting me, or whatever other rationalizations you have to tell yourselves. None of this was right. It doesn't excuse either of you lying to me," she said angrily.

"You're right, of course, Tessie. It's hard to change an old dog. I hope you believe it when I tell you, I was trying to do the right thing, but I just made things worse, apparently," James said.

"What do you mean?" Tessa asked suspiciously.

"I was worried about the story breaking, not that I thought you were in any direct danger. But I knew things had gone bad between you and Jonas, that you weren't speaking. At first, I thought that was because Jonas was irked about me firing him, and taking it out on you. But then I was put in the picture about this whole scandal possibly breaking, and it was a chance for me to try to make amends. It made sense that Jonas was the only one who you would let close, so I used that to get you two…together again."

Jonas and Tessa were shocked silent for a few minutes, until Tessa stuttered.

"Are you saying…you were…*matchmaking?*"

"Well, I don't know about that. But I was aware you were miserable when he wouldn't see you, and that was my fault. I didn't know how Howie had interjected the rest, until I learned about the scam. I thought, if I could get you together, just for a night, or a few hours, and if nature took its course…then maybe you would be all right."

"Nature taking its course?" Tessa squeaked, and

Jonas also settled back against the bed pillows, absorbing this new information.

"So you were never out to drive us apart? You were trying to…push us together?" Jonas asked, finding it hard to believe.

"That's the gist of it, yes. But when I spoke to Tessa earlier, before I landed, it was clear it hadn't gone well, because she found out I was involved. I knew that would anger her, and not put you in a good position, either," James said to Jonas.

Jonas shook his head, incredulous.

"I don't know what to say," he said honestly, seeing the senator stand.

"I do," Tessa said, standing and gathering her purse.

"I'm so tired of all this. Of the manipulation, the lying. It sounds like your intentions were good, mostly, Dad, but it doesn't change much. Jonas still thought the worst of me, and you did nothing to dissuade him."

She took a breath, continuing, "Then, when you deemed we should be together, you tried to put us together hoping nature would take its course?" she said, clearly seething.

"I can't trust either one of you because no one has been honest with me from the start. You clearly care more about what each other thinks, and you just move me back and forth like some…pawn."

"Tessie, that's simply not true. You need to—" James started, his voice stern.

"No. You need to back off, Dad. You need to stop manipulating my life and everyone else's."

Jonas's heart sank, though he couldn't blame her. She was right. He should have been honest with her from the start, at least as much as he could be, given James's manipulations.

"I do love you, Jonas," she said, making his heart race. "But I can't do this right now. Neither of you have treated me well, with honesty or respect. I can't be in a relationship that doesn't have either of those things, with either of you."

"Tessie—" James tried again, but Jonas stopped him.

"It's okay, James. She's right. If I could do this all again...I don't know. I would do it differently, I hope. But...I understand," he said to Tessa.

"I need some time. To process all this."

"Take as much as you need. I'll be waiting, if you want me," Jonas said, echoing the thing she had said to him when she came to his apartment the day before. He knew it was the right thing to do, to let her go, but he felt vulnerable and raw as she walked out, and wished the senator would leave, too.

"Don't worry, Jonas. I know my girl. She'll come around."

"I'm not sure you do know her, James. Not the way you should. Maybe that's something you should consider changing, if she gives you the chance," Jonas said. "I know I will. I'd like to get dressed and get the hell out of here. Could you leave, please?"

Jonas felt the senator's hand on his shoulder, and then watched him walk to the door.

He dressed and buzzed the nurse that he was ready to go.

It would have been one of the happiest days of his life, getting his sight back, if he knew he was ever going to see Tessa again. As it was, everything was still gray.

TESSA'S MIND WAS REELING, and when she walked out the room, she looked around for Lydia, feeling deflated when she couldn't find her. No one was there, and she assumed they had all flown the coop after leaving her and Jonas alone.

No matter, she could take a cab home. She just wanted to sleep, and to have some time to process everything in her head, and her heart.

Jonas said he loved her. She thought she loved him, but did that matter when things were so messed up?

Checking her watch, she saw it was close to noon, and wondered if Kate had been discharged yet. Making her way to her friend's floor, she found what felt like a party going on in Kate's room.

Kate was in a chair, dressed and obviously ready to leave, smiling and holding court with several other visitors. Tessa recognized Betty and several of the women from the neighborhood who came over for Sunday cards at Kate's. They all smiled when they saw her, and ushered her into the room, though she now had a few second thoughts too late.

"Tessa! I told you not to worry about me today," Kate admonished when Tessa walked in and said hello, giving Kate a hug and a kiss on the cheek. "You did more than enough last night, and you must be exhausted," she said with a mischievous wink.

"I'm fine, Kate. And I am so happy to see you're doing well. You gave us a real scare last night."

She said hello to Betty, and the other women, but suddenly, Tessa really wanted to go home. The thought that she had just walked away from Jonas, and the urge to run back to him, was confusing her.

"Where is your young man?" Betty asked. "He's a strapping fellow. Very handsome, like a movie star. I bet he's a tiger in the sack," she said, making Tessa cough in surprise.

"I trust you had a nice ride home last night?" Kate interjected with a chuckle. "The limo seats are *very* comfortable, don't you think?"

Tessa's cheeks warmed as she remembered just how comfortable they were.

"Yes, thank you so much, Kate. It was completely unnecessary, but it very considerate of you, and Collins is so sweet," she said, the memories of the night before coming back before she could finish.

Tessa put her hand to her mouth to hide the sudden, choking sensation of tears that clogged her throat. She turned away, feeling stupid, and also not wanting to upset Kate. Why was she losing it now? She should have gone straight home. Her nerves were raw after everything that had happened.

She wanted so much to be able to believe Jonas, and her father, too. She wanted the two most important men in her life to be part of it, but not in the way they had been doing.

"Oh, Tessa! What's wrong?" Kate asked with great concern, hearing her muffled sob, and suddenly Tessa was surrounded. The other women flanked her, making sure she was okay. She had to laugh and cry at the same time, and they all patted her back, urging her to sit down.

"I'm so s-sorry. I'm just tired. It's been a very long night."

"Hmm, I think there's more to it than that," Kate said. "What happened? What did *he* do? Did he break your heart? And here I thought he was such a nice young man."

Tessa waved her hand as if to wave off Kate's concern,

and grabbed a tissue with the other, trying to get hold of herself so she could stop feeling foolish. Something about sitting here with these wonderful, caring women kept the tears flowing. In so many ways, she was closer to them than she was to her own family, and that made her sad, too.

"I'm not sure we can be together," Tessa said, choking up again. "It's such an awful mess."

"There's an answer for everything. It probably just seems bad right now. Tell us what happened," Betty urged kindly.

"I think I should go," she said, standing. "I don't want to bother you all with this, and it looks like you have more than enough help to get home, so if you don't mind, Kate, I can just—"

"You're not going anywhere when you are so upset," Kate said adamantly, and the other women agreed, gently forcing Tessa back into the chair.

Betty went out into the hall, coming in a few seconds later with a cup of tea, handing it to her.

"This will help, even if it's a bit weak," she said, patting Tessa's hand. "If we were home, I would put something stronger in it, but for now this will have to do."

"So spill your guts, Tessa. We want to hear the whole story," Kate said. "Don't leave anything out."

Tessa sighed and sipped her tea. It was clear that she wasn't going to be able to leave until she told them what happened, although she definitely left out the sexier parts of her night. Somehow she just couldn't imagine telling her octogenarian friends about her sex life.

When she finished, they all stared at her in clear disbelief.

"Well, that's a better story than all the nighttime TV I watched this week," Betty said.

Kate reached for Tessa's hand. "Tessa, you are in a very difficult spot, being someone who is loved too much by the men in your life."

Tessa drew back. "I'm sorry. I'm not exactly getting that feeling."

"Your father obviously loves you very much," she said. "But in the wrong way, as men, and parents, so often do. It's a tough job, being a parent, and children sometimes need to be forgiving. But it's never too late to learn, and it sounds like he tried, at least, to do the right thing."

"But—" Tessa tried to interject.

"And your Jonas…well, we all know about *men*," she said with a sigh, and the other women murmured agreement.

"I was reading an article in *Cosmo* that said men are like cats, not dogs," Betty said, and they all looked at her, wondering how she had made that connection.

"Well, it makes sense. Domestic dogs are not like wild dogs, wolves, et cetera—house dogs aren't in touch with their wild instincts. But cats, no matter the size, are all the same. The domestic house cat has the same behavior as the lion—cats are very primal."

Tessa listened politely, trying to follow.

"Men who are in love will rely very much on primal reflexes, their baser instincts. Just like cats. They are hunters. They possess, but they also protect what they see as theirs," Betty explained.

"I'm sorry, I don't understand," Tessa said, frowning and trying to digest Betty's rather convoluted point, but also that she read *Cosmo*.

"Men show love in several ways. One way is through

sex. Another is through providing for those they care about. Another protecting them, at any cost. It goes back to caveman times," Betty said. "But they have all that testosterone flying around in their brains, and sometimes, well, they just get carried away. They forget we're adult people who can make our own decisions."

"So what you're saying is that both of them think they are protecting me?"

She knew that, she was just sick and tired of their methods. Tessa didn't want to be protected. She wanted respect, honesty and love.

"Yes, in a nutshell, and they are being complete asses about it, but that's as old as time, too. No one is perfect. And you said they both had things in the past that colored their perspectives. As did you," said Kate.

"What do you mean?"

"You were wrong about your father's motives, too. He was trying to get you together with Jonas, albeit he didn't do a great job of it, but he wasn't trying to do what he did to you in college, driving the man you loved away. But your past experience made you see things a certain way, too."

"I saw a show the other day," Betty interjected. "The psychologist had a couple with similar problems, and he asked them if they wanted to be happy, or if they wanted to be right."

"I think there's room for both," Tessa said stubbornly, seeing their points, but a little surprised that her women friends didn't see her perspective more clearly.

Or maybe they saw it very clearly.

"Tessa, you said your father never wanted you to open your shop, but now he sees what a success it is. He was obviously able to see what a good match you are with your Jonas, too," Kate said.

"I suppose. But the problem with this theory is that it means neither one of them is considering me an adult who is able to make her own decisions. I don't think I like that," Tessa said.

"Oh, believe me, they know. But for fathers, their little girls never grow up, and for Jonas, well…love scrambles people's brains." Kate smiled patiently. "But they can't change if you walk away from them. And that won't make you too happy, either, will it?"

"I can't think straight at all, about any of this."

"That's why we get so confused when we try to think our way out of these things. You know the answer, in your heart. Strong men like Jonas, and your father, for that matter, are not attracted to weak women," Kate said. "They both let you walk away. The ball is in your court. Follow your heart."

Tessa absorbed the women's advice. If she were to truly follow her heart, she knew exactly what she needed to do. Could it really be that easy? Was she just letting her pride get in the way of being happy?

It seemed so stupid.

"Kate, it does seem like you have more than enough help here. Do you mind if I leave you for today? I have… something I have to do."

Kate's eyes sparkled with interest as she gestured Tessa forward for a hug and whispered in her ear.

"Don't let him get away this time."

12

JONAS TURNED AS the door to the back room of the office opened, and he saw Garrett approach where the brothers had congregated to catch up.

"Lunch," he said approvingly as the aroma of food permeated the space. His sense of smell was still serving him well, but he was hungry for everything he could see, which, granted, at this point, wasn't much. Mostly blurry blobs moving around, shadows and shapes, but he absorbed every nuance completely, eager for his full range of vision to return.

Matt said he should be back to his full eyesight within a week, but that he might need some glasses, depending on how well his vision recovered. Jonas was fine with that. Anything was better than the complete darkness he'd been living in.

"Chinese. I didn't get breakfast, and I'm starving."

Several minutes later, as they consumed the food with no small bit of teasing about Jonas missing his target as he tried to eat the noodles and chunks of meat in the lo mein he loved—he felt more renewed and ready to dig in again. Irish purred profusely on the floor next to where Jonas sat, content to have all of them there, and happy with whatever chunks of food were being offered.

"Irish really likes that pork lo mein," Ely observed.

"He has good taste."

"Anyone know where Ely took off to?" Jonas asked, reaching down to scratch the cat behind the ears, rewarded with even louder purring.

"Any egg rolls left?" he asked.

"Let me get that for you," Chance said matter-of-factly, putting an egg roll into his hand. "He took off with the tattooed chick, Tessa's friend."

"Lydia?" Jonas said, surprised.

"They were heading to the hospital cafeteria, but that was the last I saw of them. Maybe Ely got lucky," Chance said, and Jonas could almost see his younger brother's grin.

Jonas wasn't completely happy to hear that.

"Lydia's a friend," he said, sending his brother a look. "She doesn't deserve to be Ely's rebound lay," he muttered, hoping that wasn't what his brother was doing.

It didn't seem possible. Lydia and Ely were about as different as he could imagine.

"Rebound?" Chance asked. "What did I miss?"

Ely had told Garrett and Jonas in the hosptial about the encounter with Chloe. Jonas had wanted to talk about anything other than his own issues, and noticed right away that his younger brother was out of sorts.

"She was getting married?" Chance said, clearly outraged. "That sucks."

"Yeah."

"How about you, Gar? You never said how your night went last night," Jonas prompted.

"I helped Mel with her flooding, and then I went home. Nothing to tell," his older brother reported. "It seems like you guys were getting into enough hot water for all of us combined."

"That's too bad. I like Melissa. She's had a thing for you for a while."

"She's just a friend. And I'm not interested in going there," Garrett said in the older-brother voice he used when he was telling his brothers to back off.

"It's been three years now, Gar," Jonas said gently.

"I know how long it's been, Jon. Eat your lunch."

Jonas nodded. He wasn't in the habit of poking at his brother's wounds, but maybe his own feelings about Tessa had him wondering whether any of them would find happiness in love.

He ached, and set down the egg roll that Chance had given him, suddenly not hungry at all.

"You okay?" Garrett asked.

"Yeah. Tired."

"And you miss her."

"Yeah."

"You could call. Go to her," Garrett suggested.

Jonas shook his head. "No. It has to be on her terms, what she wants, even if it's to be left alone. I really screwed it up the first time, so I'm just going to have to wait."

He was hurting, missing her more than he had ever missed anything, including his vision. But he meant what he said. It had to be up to her.

It did feel good to talk about it with his brothers, though. One thing he had learned with Tessa, and from being blind, was that he didn't need to do it all on his own. Part of that was probably because he knew now that his sight was returning, but also because accepting help in general was suddenly not such a huge deal. It cemented his connections with others, and he'd never really thought about it that way before.

The defensiveness he'd felt for the last month seemed to go away, and it was a relief. He felt stronger for having shared his problems with his brothers—and for his time with Tessa—not weaker.

"Well, maybe you won't have to wait as long as you think," Garrett said while unwrapping a fortune cookie.

Jonas took a bite of his egg roll, and chewed thoughtfully. "I'll wait as long as it takes."

"I'm glad to hear that," someone said behind him, and he immediately knew it was Tessa's voice.

He heard his brother chuckle. Garrett had known she was there.

"Tessa?"

"Yes," she said.

He felt her hand on his shoulder, and he reached up, covering it with his own.

"How long have you been there?"

"Long enough," she said, and he could hear the tears in her voice. "Thank you," she whispered, leaning down to plant a kiss on his cheek.

It was all Jonas could do not to pull her down into his arms, and not let go. But he let her set the lead.

"For what?"

"For understanding," she said simply.

Jonas was silent with surprise. A part of him was sure she'd never come back, never forgive him. He tightened his grips on her hand, to make sure she was really there.

"Here, have a seat," Chance said at the same time Jonas heard Garrett offering his chair, too, and the guys scrambled around him as they all tried to make Tessa welcome and comfortable.

Jonas smiled, and heard Tessa chuckling and thanking them as she took a seat beside Jonas, her hand still wrapped in his.

"I'm sorry about this morning. The note, scaring you. I wish it had gone down differently," he said.

"No, that's the point, Jonas. I'm so tired of everyone trying to protect me from everything," she said, tilting her forehead against his. "I know it's your job, and your nature, to do that, but I don't want you, my father, or anyone protecting me when it means not being honest or letting me know what's going on in your head, or your heart."

Before he could say anything else, his brothers, as if coordinated ahead of time, rose and briskly left the room.

"There's one thing you're missing."

"What's that?" she asked.

"I did want to tell you, and I should have. About my blindness, the job—but I was afraid. It wasn't as much about protecting you as protecting myself," he said with no small amount of self-disgust.

"How so?"

"Howie's threats were an issue, but it was easier to use them as an excuse and to pretend it was all your fault than to face you and have you see me as…diminished, I suppose."

"You thought the loss of your vision would matter to me?" she said in surprise. "How could you think that?"

"Because I felt that way about myself, not just because

I was blind, but because I had let the attacker get the upper hand, had failed to protect you...I don't know, it all wrapped up together in some way in my head. And then, when your dad offered me a chance to be with you again, I took it, but the lie ate at me. I knew it was wrong, but I did it anyway, because I knew when you found out, you'd be gone."

"So instead, you decided to leave first?"

"I thought I could try to find a way to make things right."

"You're doing that right now. But I was part of this, too," she said. "I saw what I wanted to see, followed my own selfish desires—"

"I love your selfish desires," he said.

"You know what I mean. We have a lot of time to make up for...just getting to know each other. Really know each other. I want to know everything about you."

He definitely loved her, and leaned in, toward her scent.

"I can't believe you're here," he said, sliding a hand up into her hair, pulling her in for a kiss, feeling as if it had been days, weeks, instead of just a few hours.

Her hands framed his face in a tender gesture as she kissed him back, and the mood wasn't one so much of desire—though he certainly wanted her—as it was of... gratitude.

And something much, much deeper, he realized.

"I do love you, Tessa," Jonas confessed, the words so easy to say it almost surprised him.

She let out a shaky breath. "That's all I needed to hear. I love you, too. And we'll make this all work out, somehow."

"What about your father?" he said.

She laughed. "Jonas, he clearly likes the idea of you with me, so no worries there. I like that idea, too," she said. "But I'll talk with him, too. Maybe this can be a fresh start for me and him. His heart was in the right place, and maybe it always has been, but I was too defensive to see it."

"I know that feeling," he murmured against her throat, suddenly wishing they were alone, not here with his brothers nearby.

Where he had ever gotten the idea that she needed his protection in the first place now mystified him. She'd taken out the attacker in her apartment, and she'd taken on her father, and him. She'd been strong enough to tell them to leave, to stand on her own and still to come back, to forgive.

Her lips found his again, and it was long, rich moments before either of them spoke again. Jonas saw the shape of the window behind her, and lifted his hand to follow the shadowed contour of her head.

Soon, though hardly soon enough, he'd be able to see her again, fully and clearly, but until then, he was more than happy to use his hands, and all his senses, to compensate for what his eyes missed.

ELY OPENED HIS EYES, not quite sure what he was looking at as he stared upward at the brick red ceiling. He'd been in so many places over the last week, he'd lost track.

Red satin sheets rubbed against his naked skin, and then he remembered.

Lydia.

Pushing up on the bed, he heard voices sounding as if they were coming from the floor below, and it came back to him.

Going without any sleep for forty-eight hours had finally caught up with him, and he'd completely passed out—after discovering that Lydia did, indeed, have tattoos in places where only lovers could see.

They'd ended up going for a drink instead of for coffee. A couple of drinks, actually. Not smart when he was already tired, but he was sick of worrying about it. He'd been raw inside from seeing Chloe, and even told Lydia the whole sordid story.

She'd taken him by the hand, took him home. Undressed him.

Told him it was just for the moment.

He'd needed…something. Someone to wash away Chloe's touch, and Lydia had done a fine and thorough job of that. She was the complete opposite of Chloe in every way, and that was what he'd needed.

He rubbed his wrists, noting a few bruises.

Right. The handcuffs.

Sliding off the side of the bed, he looked around, noting how her bedroom reflected the woman. Leather clothing hung over a chair, and an assortment of S and M paraphernalia adorned the walls.

He pushed past the black lace curtain that surrounded the huge four-poster bed, and took in the classic French boudoir decor mixed with modern-day dungeon.

It was feminine, sexy and…more than a little kinky. Black and white nudes were framed on the walls, though the faces weren't visible, and he wondered if it was Lydia in the photos. He looked at them, finding them incredibly erotic, which was probably the point.

It was all new to him, and suddenly, for all of his experience, he felt completely vanilla, as if there were a whole lot of sexual horizons this Marine had never explored.

Lydia had helped him see that. Why did he want to get tied down—so to speak—with one person?

He was an idiot to think he wanted anything long term. He'd seen his brother Garrett suffer a terrible loss, and who knew how things would end up with Jonas. He'd almost lost his sight, and his life, over Tessa.

And Chloe had proved that his romantic notions were an illusion.

Lydia seemed to understand that, too. As she said, they only had the moment. It was how he was going to live his life from now on, he thought, hiking up his jeans and slipping his shirt on.

Walking out into the main room of the apartment, he found nothing like the bedroom. The walls were painted in strong colors, but there weren't any chains or shackles on the walls. In fact, the place could belong to a librarian, with all the books that lined the walls.

He heard voices coming from below, where she was probably working. She'd left some doughnuts out on the counter with a carton of orange juice, but he wasn't hungry. Checking the back, he was happy to find stairs leading down to a rear alley.

No need to disturb her while she was with a client.

Finding his way out, Ely put everything from the previous twenty-four hours or so behind him.

Epilogue

November, three months later

"ARE YOU sure you're okay?" Tessa asked again as Lydia helped her manage her dress.

"You're the bride—aren't I supposed to be asking you that?"

Tessa laughed, but she wasn't at all nervous. She'd been so excited to finally be marrying Jonas that she couldn't wait to walk down the aisle.

"I know something happened with you and Ely, Lydia. You two avoid each other like the plague. What did he do?"

Lydia smiled, but didn't meet Tessa's eyes.

"Nothing that I didn't want him to." The tone of her voice communicated that she wasn't going to say more. "You look perfect. I'm not such a fan of white, as you know, but this is one of the prettiest dresses I have ever seen."

They were doing everything very traditionally for the wedding—in deference to their parents' wishes—though it was a small ceremony. Jonas's parents were wonderful, and she had loved them immediately. Emily

Berringer had wasted no time taking Tessa under her wing and helping her make wedding plans, for which Tessa was so grateful. It was overwhelming, in a good way, but she loved the Berringers' hands-on way of doing everything.

There would be some media at the event, a few hand-selected reporters and one photographer from the paper that her father had approved. Tessa was okay with it—it was part of being the daughter of a politician.

The pretty Quaker church that was set among the hills of the Pennsylvania countryside was perfect, their guests few but special to her and Jonas.

Tessa looked in the mirror, studying the dress. The full-length silk felt wonderful against her skin. It was fitted, strapless, with hundreds of tiny pearls and rhine-stones arranged in flowering patterns that caught the light as she moved. The design was in some ways plain, but stunning. She wore only gardenias in her hair, and her bouquet matched the special scent she had created just for the wedding—and the honeymoon.

She'd blended something special for Jonas, too, a more subtle, masculine scent that would promote stamina, she thought with a smile. He was going to need it. Not that she had any complaints.

If she thought the sex the night of the blackout had been intense, what they had shared since openly declaring their feelings for each other had been off the charts. She couldn't wait to see what new levels of pleasure marriage would bring. She knew that all the cynical comments people made about being lifetime partners with someone were wrong, at least for them.

Far from losing the heat of the initial meeting, everything just got more intense the closer they became, not less so.

She shifted in the dress, slightly, her nipples beading in anticipation.

"Geez, you're worse than me," Lydia said, laughing and meeting her eyes in the mirror. "You're already thinking about the honeymoon, aren't you?"

Tessa grinned. "Guilty as charged. I mean, I'm looking forward to this, to marrying Jonas, but the wedding is really for our parents, and everyone else. I just want him."

"You two are amazing. You almost make me believe it can happen," Lydia said. "Though it's not for me."

"It might be, when you meet the right man."

"You know my philosophy on that."

Tessa did, and it made her a little sad. She hated being one of those brides who went around wanting to see all her friends married, too, but she wanted Lydia to be as happy as she was, someday.

"Jonas is going to go blind again when he sees you, you're so gorgeous," Lydia, her only attendant, said, stepping back.

"Well, let's hope not," Tessa said with a smile. She had some treats planned for Jonas, and he very much needed to be able to see.

Uncharacteristically sentimental, the women hugged, and Tessa was determined not to cry, or she'd ruin her makeup again for the second time that morning.

It had been bad enough when Chance, Ely and Garrett had all come to see her and welcome her to the family, each presenting her with a small gift of their own.

She'd noticed, though, how when Ely came in, Lydia had gone, the two not even sharing a glance.

"Ready?" Lydia said.

"So very, very ready," Tessa replied, taking her

flowers and heading out to meet her father, who was giving her away.

As the music cued, and Tessa saw Jonas at the other end of the aisle, heart-stoppingly handsome in his tux, she swallowed hard.

Oh, these were the nerves everyone talked about, she thought, freezing for a second.

But then Jonas smiled, and her father took her arm in his, and everything was okay again.

Lydia led the way, and took her place on the left side of the judge—a prestigious friend of her father's—and Garrett stood on the right with his brother.

She knew this was hard for Gar, her heart breaking. The last wedding he had attended had been his own.

As she came closer to Jonas, she had eyes only for him, and felt her cheeks warm again as his eyes landed on her, and took her in.

His gaze consumed her, as it so often did. Even though he had had his vision for more than a month, she still caught him staring, as if he couldn't take in enough.

He took her hand, raised it to his lips, and the world came down to the two of them for the next few minutes.

LATER, EVERYONE CONGREGATED in the hall next to the church for drinks and some food, and Tessa looked around for where her new husband had disappeared to.

"Gar, do you know where Jonas went?" she asked her new brother-in-law.

"He's getting his gift for you."

She raised her eyebrows, wondering what he could be working on that would be so mysterious. Smiling, she invited Garrett to dance with her, which he was pleased to do.

She noted Ely dancing with the woman he'd invited as his date, and who was clearly one of his recent string of conquests. Tessa knew Jonas was worried about his younger brother, who was normally quite conservative.

Chance, who was the complete opposite, was dancing with three partners, never one to be outdone.

Lydia sat chatting with Tessa's father, and Tessa frowned, but turned her attention back to Garrett.

"So Jonas said that you're leaving, too, after the reception?" Tessa asked Garrett.

"Yep. It's slow right now, and a good friend on the West Coast is getting married, so I'm going to go out there to the wedding, and then take a month for vacation. I've never been to California," he said. "It should be fun."

"Sounds great. Thanks for being Jonas's best man," she said gently. "I know it must bring back memories."

"Just good ones," he said, smiling at her, but his eyes were still a little sad.

"You could have brought a date, too," she said, no subtle way to broach the topic. By now, Garrett probably qualified for a monastery.

"I'm fine, Tessa. Better than fine. I'm thrilled for you guys. I have to admit, weddings are not my favorite events, but it's been a while, and I'm a big boy."

"I know, it's just that…we want you to be happy."

"I was," he said, and then shook his head. "I mean, I am," he corrected. "Besides, there are only so many perfect women in the world, and Jonas just took one of the last ones."

Tessa reached up and planted a kiss on his cheek.

"Hey, I think your gift from Jonas is waiting," Garrett said, grinning as they were interrupted by a loud, growling noise.

"What is *that?*" she exclaimed, and saw everyone going to the double doors at the front of the hall.

"It's his other love," Garrett said laughingly. "Go on," Garrett urged. "It's about time you two meet."

She looked at him curiously and made her way forward, walked through as the small group parted down the center to allow her access. When she reached the door at the top of the steps, she stopped.

Surprise didn't cover what she saw.

Jonas. Dressed completely in black leather, sitting on a huge, black motorcycle, smiling up at her.

He looked...dangerous. A thrill ran down her spine.

He'd mentioned the bike, but hadn't ridden it since getting his sight back, and she'd wondered why.

The bike was decorated with Just Married decor, and he dropped the kickstand, taming the roaring noise as he hopped off and met her at the top at the door.

"Ready to leave on our honeymoon?" he said, taking her hands in his.

"On that?" she asked, looking at the bike apprehensively.

"You'll like it," he said, nuzzling her ear. "I promise."

She wasn't so sure.

"We're taking the Harley to the airport, and then we have a private charter to St. Thomas, a gift from both of our parents. From there we'll take a sailboat that will sail us to a private cottage on a beach in Anguilla, and down through several of the other islands."

Tessa was so moved, and so surprised, she turned to hug her new in-laws, and her father, who hugged her back, and, she suspected, was having just a teeny bit of a hard time letting go.

But he had been so good about everything. Their relationship had never been better.

She'd had to try to pack without really knowing where his parents were shipping their luggage off to, keeping it a surprise, but she wasn't prepared for this.

"I thought we could keep up our tradition of using as many modes of transportation as possible," Jonas said, hugging her close. "And discovering how we might take advantage of them."

She checked out the way the leather hugged his body and a tingle raced down her spine. She had no doubt they would find a lot of new erotic possibilities along the way.

"But I can't ride that…not in this," she said, looking down at her dress.

"That's where my gift comes in," Lydia said happily, appearing on the step and pushing a box into her hands. "Open it."

Tess opened the huge, heavy box and found a succulent leather jacket, skirt and boots inside, along with some very sexy lingerie. Jonas smiled broadly as she closed the box before others could see the naughty accoutrements.

"Go change," he whispered in her ear. "I can't wait to see you in this outfit, and to get you out of it."

Cheers went up as Jonas took her in his arms for a deep, consuming kiss that left Tessa more than willing to leave as soon as possible.

The wedding had been wonderful, but she wanted to get her new husband alone. They would be making more than one fantasy come true on their honeymoon, and she had a few surprises in store for him, as well.

JONAS WASN'T SURE he had ever known such a perfect moment as he did easing down the road on his Harley, Tessa pressed up tight against his back, the fall colors brilliant as they rode down the highway.

He pulled to the side of the road, into a tree-lined alcove, where he stopped the bike.

"Is something wrong?"

"No. I just need to be alone with my wife," he said, turning and lifting her hand to his mouth, loving the sight of his rings on her finger. "We have some time, and I thought you might like to experiment with some of the more creative things people can do on a motorcycle seat," he said, pulling her close and taking her lips in a hot kiss.

"I have to admit, the vibration has been quite… stimulating," she said, and smiled as he unzipped the tight leather and her bare breasts fell free. The cool air tightened her nipples invitingly, and he dipped in for a taste.

Jonas groaned, appreciating her choice to forgo any of the lingerie that Lydia had bought her. He had a feeling they might not make it all the way to the airport, and had been thankful to find the protected spot.

His hands slid up her thighs under the leather, and discovered that she wasn't wearing anything under the skirt, either. The wide seat of the motorcycle meant her legs were already open to him, and he drew a finger along her sex, finding her wet already. His cock pressed against his own leather, needing to be inside her.

He caressed her more deeply, watching her head fall back in the dappled sunlight as he made her come with just his touch. She was so responsive, he had a hard time keeping control.

But his wife had plans of her own. Reaching forward, she cleverly released the front of his leathers, his erection full and ready, straining toward her.

"Someone might see," she said, knowing how to make his pulse race.

"The trees are hiding us, but maybe we had better make this one quick, just in case," he agreed, pulling her up from straddling the seat to his lap, sinking her down over him until they were completely connected.

She wrapped her arms around him tightly as he turned the bike back on, letting it idle and purr beneath them in the most delicious way.

"Oh, my, that's very nice," she said breathlessly, and he had to admit to enjoying the subtle vibration before he gripped her hips and sought his climax more energetically.

He watched her again, fighting not to close his eyes through his own climax as she cried out, biting her lip and giving herself over to it. She was so beautiful, and she was his.

After a few moments, he set her gently aside, kissing her tenderly as he zipped her back up. "I love you, wife."

"I love you, husband. And just in case you think I forgot, I have a surprise for you when we get where we're going."

"What's that?"

"My gift for you is with our luggage, so it will have to wait until tomorrow, but let's just say I bought something to make both of our 'in the dark' fantasies come true," she said, adding, "You said you'd be more than willing to watch…and now that you can…"

Jonas was sure he had died and gone to heaven.

"I think we'll find a lot of new things to do on the boat, and maybe even on the plane," she teased, and his heart raced thinking about it.

"I already have a few ideas," he said, holding her tight for one more kiss.

She handed him his helmet, and slid from his lap to the seat. "Let's go. There are only so many hours in a day, and so many fantasies to explore."

"We'd best get started then," he agreed, looking forward to every single one.

* * * * *

COMING NEXT MONTH

Available June 28, 2011

#621 BY INVITATION ONLY
Lori Wilde, Wendy Etherington, Jillian Burns

#622 TAILSPIN
Uniformly Hot!
Cara Summers

#623 WICKED PLEASURES
The Pleasure Seekers
Tori Carrington

#624 COWBOY UP
Sons of Chance
Vicki Lewis Thompson

#625 JUST LET GO...
Harts of Texas
Kathleen O'Reilly

#626 KEPT IN THE DARK
24 Hours: Blackout
Heather MacAllister

HBCNM0611

REQUEST YOUR FREE BOOKS!
2 FREE NOVELS PLUS 2 FREE GIFTS!

red-hot reads!

YES! Please send me 2 FREE Harlequin® Blaze® novels and my 2 FREE gifts (gifts are worth about $10). After receiving them, if I don't wish to receive any more books, I can return the shipping statement marked "cancel." If I don't cancel, I will receive 6 brand-new novels every month and be billed just $4.24 per book in the U.S. or $4.71 per book in Canada. That's a saving of at least 15% off the cover price. It's quite a bargain. Shipping and handling is just 50¢ per book in the U.S. and 75¢ per book in Canada.* I understand that accepting the 2 free books and gifts places me under no obligation to buy anything. I can always return a shipment and cancel at any time. Even if I never buy another book, the two free books and gifts are mine to keep forever.

151/351 HDN FC4T

Name _____ (PLEASE PRINT) _____

Address _____ Apt. # _____

City _____ State/Prov. _____ Zip/Postal Code _____

Signature (if under 18, a parent or guardian must sign) _____

Mail to the **Reader Service:**
IN U.S.A.: P.O. Box 1867, Buffalo, NY 14240-1867
IN CANADA: P.O. Box 609, Fort Erie, Ontario L2A 5X3

Not valid for current subscribers to Harlequin Blaze books.

Want to try two free books from another line?
Call 1-800-873-8635 or visit www.ReaderService.com.

* Terms and prices subject to change without notice. Prices do not include applicable taxes. Sales tax applicable in N.Y. Canadian residents will be charged applicable taxes. Offer not valid in Quebec. This offer is limited to one order per household. All orders subject to credit approval. Credit or debit balances in a customer's account(s) may be offset by any other outstanding balance owed by or to the customer. Please allow 4 to 6 weeks for delivery. Offer available while quantities last.

Your Privacy—The Reader Service is committed to protecting your privacy. Our Privacy Policy is available online at www.ReaderService.com or upon request from the Reader Service.

We make a portion of our mailing list available to reputable third parties that offer products we believe may interest you. If you prefer that we not exchange your name with third parties, or if you wish to clarify or modify your communication preferences, please visit us at www.ReaderService.com/consumerschoice or write to us at Reader Service Preference Service, P.O. Box 9062, Buffalo, NY 14269. Include your complete name and address.

HBII

USA TODAY *bestselling author B.J. Daniels takes you on a trip to Whitehorse, Montana, and the Chisholm Cattle Company.*

RUSTLED

Available July 2011 from Harlequin Intrigue.

As the dust settled, Dawson got his first good look at the rustler. A pair of big Montana sky-blue eyes glared up at him from a face framed by blond curls.

A woman rustler?

"You have to let me go," she hollered as the roar of the stampeding cattle died off in the distance.

"So you can finish stealing my cattle? I don't think so." Dawson jerked the woman to her feet.

She reached for the gun strapped to her hip hidden under her long barn jacket.

He grabbed the weapon before she could, his eyes narrowing as he assessed her. "How many others are there?" he demanded, grabbing a fistful of her jacket. "I think you'd better start talking before I tear into you."

She tried to fight him off, but he was on to her tricks and pinned her to the ground. He was suddenly aware of the soft curves beneath the jean jacket she wore under her coat.

"You have to listen to me." She ground out the words from between her gritted teeth. "You have to let me go. If you don't they will come back for me and they will kill you. There are too many of them for you to fight off alone. You won't stand a chance and I don't want your blood on my hands."

"I'm touched by your concern for me. Especially after you just tried to pull a gun on me."

"I wasn't going to shoot you."

Dawson hauled her to her feet and walked her the rest of the way to his horse. Reaching into his saddlebag, he pulled out a length of rope.

"You can't tie me up."

He pulled her hands behind her back and began to tie her wrists together.

"If you let me go, I can keep them from coming back," she said. "You have my word." She let out an unladylike curse. "I'm just trying to save your sorry neck."

"And I'm just going after my cattle."

"Don't you mean your boss's cattle?"

"Those cattle are mine."

"*You're* a Chisholm?"

"Dawson Chisholm. And you are…?"

"Everyone calls me Jinx."

He chuckled. "I can see why."

Bronco busting, falling in love…it's all in a day's work.
Look for the rest of their story in

RUSTLED

Available July 2011 from Harlequin Intrigue
wherever books are sold.

THE NOTORIOUS
WOLFES

A powerful dynasty,
where secrets and scandal never sleep!

Eight siblings, blessed with wealth, but denied the one
thing they wanted—a father's love. Haunted by their
past and driven to succeed, the Wolfes scattered to the
far corners of the globe. It's said that even the blackest
of souls can be healed by the purest of love....

But can the dynasty rise again?

Beginning July 2011

A NIGHT OF SCANDAL—*Sarah Morgan*
THE DISGRACED PLAYBOY—*Caitlin Crews*
THE STOLEN BRIDE—*Abby Green*
THE FEARLESS MAVERICK—*Robyn Grady*
THE MAN WITH THE MONEY—*Lynn Raye Harris*
THE TROPHY WIFE—*Janette Kenny*
THE GIRL THAT LOVE FORGOT—*Jennie Lucas*
THE LONE WOLFE—*Kate Hewitt*

8 volumes to collect and treasure!

ROMANTIC
SUSPENSE

Secrets and scandal ignite in a danger-filled,
passion-fuelled new miniseries.

**Family. Lies.
Full exposure.**

When scandal erupts, threatening California Senator
Hank Kelley's career and his life, there's only one place he can
turn—the family ranch in Maple Cove, Montana. But he'll need
the help of his estranged sons and their friends to pull the family
together despite attempts on his life and pressure from a sinister
secret society, and to prevent an unthinkable tragedy that would
shake the country to its core.

Collect all 6 heart-racing tales starting July 2011 with
Private Justice
by *USA TODAY* bestselling author
MARIE FERRARELLA

Special Ops Bodyguard by **BETH CORNELISON** (August 2011)

Cowboy Under Siege by **GAIL BARRETT** (September 2011)

Rancher Under Cover by **CARLA CASSIDY** (October 2011)

Missing Mother-To-Be by **ELLE KENNEDY** (November 2011)

Captain's Call of Duty by **CINDY DEES** (December 2011)